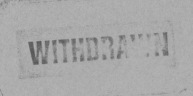

MOVIE for DOGS

ALSO BY LOIS DUNCAN

FOR YOUNGER READERS

News for Dogs
Hotel for Dogs
A Gift of Magic
I Walk at Night
Song of the Circus
The Magic of Spider Woman
Wonder Kid Meets the Evil Lunch Snatcher
The Longest Hair in the World
The Birthday Moon
The Circus Comes Home
Horses of Dreamland
From Spring to Spring
Songs from Dreamland
Chapters: My Growth as a Writer
The Terrible Tales of Happy Days School

FOR OLDER READERS

Summer of Fear
Down a Dark Hall
Don't Look Behind You
The Twisted Window
The Third Eye
I Know What You Did Last Summer
Stranger with My Face
Ransom

MOVIE FOR DOGS

BY LOIS DUNCAN

Scholastic Inc.

NEW YORK   TORONTO   LONDON   AUCKLAND

SYDNEY   MEXICO CITY   NEW DELHI   HONG KONG

ISBN 978-0-545-10854-6

12 11 10 9 8 7 6 5 4 3 2 1   10 11 12 13 14 15/0

Printed in the U.S.A. 23
First printing, June 2010

For Matthew Daniel Walpole
with happy wishes

CHAPTER ONE

The envelope was at the top of the pile of letters under the mail slot when Andi Walker arrived home from school on Friday afternoon. When she saw the return address of Pet Lovers Press, her heart started pounding so hard that she was afraid it might pop through her chest.

For six long months she had been waiting for this very letter, rushing home from school every day to see if it had come. And finally, here it was, lying on the floor in the entrance hall, as ordinary-looking as if it were an advertisement for laundry detergent and not an announcement of the most important event of her life.

She had submitted her manuscript to the Young Author Dog Lovers Contest the past October. It was now more than halfway through April, and she had started to worry that her manuscript had been lost in the mail. Or worse, that some unscrupulous worker at the post office — not a regular employee, of course, but a substitute with a criminal background — had stolen her story and submitted it under his own name. She'd had to keep reassuring herself that such a thing would be impossible, because contestants were required to be under the age of sixteen and people that age very seldom worked for the post office.

The age restriction had not been a problem for Andi, who had written the book when she was eleven and had turned twelve in December. Despite her young age, Andi was an experienced writer. Her poetry appeared in almost every issue of the school paper, and the past summer she and her brother and two of their friends had published a newspaper for dogs called *The Bow-Wow News*. Andi had been the editor.

However, she'd never tried to write a novel before this one. When she'd seen a flier about the contest posted in the library and read that the winning story would be published by Pet Lovers Press, she'd known at once that this was the opportunity of a lifetime. The stories had to be about dogs, and Andi was a dog person. She felt sure she knew more about dogs than anyone else in the world and definitely loved them more than anybody else did. She had worked all summer writing her novel, and the day she'd mailed off the manuscript in a large envelope covered with stamps — she hadn't been sure how much postage it needed, and didn't want to risk falling short — she'd been certain her entry would win.

How could it not, when so much love and work had gone into it?

Andi bent down and picked up the envelope. Then she just stood there, enjoying the feel of it in her hands and imagining what it would be like when she opened it. She didn't want that moment to come too quickly, because once it was over, it would become part of the past. It would be like the letdown that came on Christmas afternoon, when all the gifts had been unwrapped and the paper and bows had been stuffed into a trash bag or burned in the fireplace. No matter how happy you were with the presents, the magical sense of anticipation vanished.

Suddenly, the front door flew open so hard it almost knocked her over, and her brother, Bruce, burst into the house. Bruce, who attended Elmwood Middle School, which let out later than

Elmwood Elementary, always came rushing home with two things on his mind — getting something to eat and taking his dog for a run.

"Sorry," he said as the door slammed into his sister. "Why are you standing right in the doorway? You look like you've grown roots."

"My novel, *Bobby Strikes Back*, is going to be published," Andi told him, savoring the sound of the words. "I've won the Young Author Dog Lovers Contest."

"How do you know?" Bruce asked, gesturing to the unopened envelope. "You haven't even read the letter yet."

"I must have won," Andi said. "Publishers return manuscripts in big brown envelopes. I've gotten a lot of poems and stories back from magazines, and they always come in brown envelopes. This is a regular envelope with one piece of paper in it. I can tell because it's so light. I'm going to wait until the exact right moment to open it."

"And when will that be?" Bruce asked her. His sister never ceased to bewilder him. His best friend, Tim Kelly, had little sisters who reminded Bruce of a set of dominoes — exactly alike except for the number of freckles on their upturned noses. But

Andi wasn't like anyone else he'd ever known. Personally, he couldn't imagine postponing opening a letter, especially if he knew it contained something wonderful.

"I'm going to open it at the dinner table," Andi told him. "Then Dad and Mom will reward me by taking us out for ice cream. I'm going to have a strawberry sundae."

"They'll take us out for ice cream no matter when you open that envelope," Bruce said reasonably. "They always do that when there's something to celebrate. I'm going to have a triple-dip chocolate cone."

Leaving his sister anchored to the floor in the entrance hall, he went into the kitchen and grabbed a handful of cookies from one container and a dog biscuit from another. Then he let himself out into the backyard.

"Red, come!" he called. "Snack time!"

His Irish setter, Red Rover, came bounding to greet him, his bright plume of a tail swishing back and forth so wildly that Bruce half expected the dog to take off like a helicopter.

Bruce crammed the cookies into his own mouth and held up the biscuit.

"Sit!" he said. "Say 'Please!'"

Red immediately sat and gave a short, sharp bark. His tail now pounded the ground instead of the air.

"Say 'Pretty please!'" Bruce told him, and Red barked twice.

Bruce tossed the biscuit, and Red leapt to catch it in midair. Feeding a biscuit to Red was like feeding a peanut to an elephant; it slid down his throat so fast that you knew he hadn't tasted it.

"If you want to go running, you'll have to open the gate," Bruce said. "But don't even think about doing that until I say the magic word."

The past summer, when Red had pulled free of his leash and rushed into traffic, Bruce's father had threatened to take the big dog away from him. Mr. Walker was worried that Bruce, who was small for his age, was not strong enough to control an excitable setter. He had finally agreed that Bruce could keep Red Rover if he got a book about dog training and taught the dog to obey. Bruce had taken the challenge seriously, and Red had proved to be a good student. Not only did he now obey such common commands as "come," "heel," "sit," and "paws up," he'd also learned an assortment of complicated tricks, one of which was to open the backyard gate. But he always waited for Bruce to issue the command.

Now Bruce snapped the leash onto Red's collar and shouted, "Open, sesame!" At the sound of those words, Red stood up on his hind legs and pressed his front paws against the top of the gate. Then he took the latch in his teeth and lifted it.

The gate swung open, and boy and dog raced joyfully down the alley and onto a sidewalk lined with maple trees. The bare winter branches had just begun to sprout new leaves, and the fringe of pale green was as delicate as lace against the clear blue sky. In the front yards of houses up and down the block, the first tulips and daffodils had broken through the earth, not yet an explosion of color as they would be soon, but a promise of what was to come in a matter of weeks.

Bruce always took the same route on their afternoon runs; he wanted to avoid Jerry Gordon's house, which was inconveniently located near the end of the block, next door to his father's aunt Alice. There was no way for Bruce to get around it when he visited his great-aunt, but left to himself, he always headed in the opposite direction.

With the possible exception of Jerry's cousin,

Connor, who lived in Chicago, Jerry was the worst person Bruce had ever known. Jerry had been Red Rover's original owner but had mistreated the dog so badly that Mr. Gordon had agreed to sell Red to Bruce. Jerry had never forgiven Bruce for buying Red and had used every opportunity to make both Bruce's and Red's lives miserable. It was Jerry who had caused Red to run into traffic by trying to ram him with his skateboard, and the previous summer, Jerry and Connor, who had been spending the summer in Elmwood, had come up with a dognapping scheme that had caused many innocent people a huge amount of heartache.

To make matters worse — at least, as far as Bruce was concerned — Jerry, who was his age, was four inches taller and twenty pounds heavier than he was. He was also extremely good-looking and had an angelic smile that charmed every adult he came in contact with. Bruce tried to stay as far away from him as possible.

But why am I thinking about Jerry now? he asked himself. The traumatic events of the previous summer were far behind him. Over the winter he hadn't seen Jerry much at all, except at school, where they were in the same English class. Now, as he ran with his dog in the bright April sunshine, there was no menacing whir of skateboard wheels behind them to disrupt the peace and serenity of the glorious afternoon. Red was in his element, stretching his lean, strong legs at a gallop, with his long ears streaming behind him like russet banners. From the very first moment Bruce had seen him, he had thought Red Rover was the most beautiful animal in the world.

They ran for just over a mile before Bruce reined Red in and made him turn around so they could head for home. As they neared the house, Red picked up even more speed, and Bruce had to strain to keep up with him. As much as Red loved his outings, he also loved going home to gobble up his dinner.

The backyard gate still stood open, and Bruce let go of Red's leash to allow him to race inside. Then he entered the yard himself and latched the gate behind him. When he turned to face the house, he was surprised to see Andi sitting on the back steps. Her dachshund, Bebe, was draped across her knees like a dog-shaped blanket.

The envelope from the publishing house lay open at Andi's feet, and she was holding the letter as if it were burning her fingers.

"I couldn't wait until dinner to open it," she said. "I'm glad I didn't, because it wasn't what I thought it was."

Bruce went over and sat down next to her on the steps. He had never seen his sister look so dejected.

"You didn't win." It was a statement rather than a question. "I know you're disappointed, but there's always a next time. They'll probably run the contest again next year."

"Next year's contest will be about cats," Andi said.

"Oh." Bruce could think of nothing to say to comfort her. Andi was not a cat lover. He could not imagine her writing a book about cats.

"I came in second," Andi said. "They're sending my manuscript back in a separate envelope so they can include a certificate."

"You got second place!" Bruce exclaimed, no longer feeling sorry for her. "Then what are you moping about? Second place is terrific!"

"But the winner —" Andi said. "The winner —"

She choked on the words, unable to continue.

"How old was the winner?" Bruce asked her.

"Fourteen," Andi said.

"Two years older than you? So, what can you expect? The winner's had two more years to practice writing stories."

"It isn't the age that matters," Andi said miserably. "The awful thing is the first-place winner is *Jerry Gordon*!"

CHAPTER TWO

"It can't be!" Bruce exploded. "Jerry isn't a writer!"

"We can't know that for sure," Andi said. "He's cruel and sneaky, but that doesn't mean he can't write. Maybe he wrote a story about cutting dogs' heads off."

"I guess that's possible," Bruce said, for she had made a good point. Being gifted in writing — or in anything else, for that matter — didn't necessarily make you a good person. On the other hand, he had never seen the slightest indication that Jerry was a talented writer. Whenever their English teacher assigned them an essay to write, Jerry groaned more loudly than anybody else in the class.

At dinner that night, Andi put on a good show. When their parents reacted with delight to the news that their daughter had placed second in a national contest, Andi forced her mouth into a smile so wide that it made her cheeks bulge like a chipmunk's.

"What an honor!" Mr. Walker exclaimed, beaming with pride. "Our little girl is going to be a local celebrity!"

"I don't think so," Andi said. "The first-place winner was Jerry Gordon, so he'll be the one who'll be getting all the attention."

"Jerry?" Their father could not conceal his amazement. "Well, that's a startling revelation! Who would have guessed that boy was disciplined enough to write a book? Maybe he needed a challenging activity to pass the time while he was confined to his house. His father told me he grounded Jerry for two weeks after all the trouble he and Connor got into last summer."

"Let's consider this a good sign," Mrs. Walker said hopefully. "Young people do go through phases. Now that he's out from under his cousin's bad influence, Jerry may become an entirely different person."

"I'm going to get a certificate," Andi announced, making her voice trill as if she were excited. "I'm going to frame it and hang it on the wall in my bedroom."

"Not in your bedroom — in the den, where everyone can see it!" Mr. Walker told her. "After dinner, let's go out for ice cream to celebrate!"

"Andi, why don't you call Aunt Alice and tell her the wonderful news?" Mrs. Walker suggested. "I bet she'd like to come with us. She loves celebrations."

"Tonight is Aunt Alice's bingo night," Andi said. "Besides, I'm too full for ice cream. I'd rather stay home and watch TV."

"I never thought I'd hear you say that!" her father exclaimed. "Since when is Andrea Walker too full to eat ice cream?"

"She's overexcited," Mrs. Walker said with a knowing smile. "I bet she'll change her mind when we get to the Dairy Queen."

However, Andi's appetite showed no signs of improving. She shoved her food around on her dinner plate to give the impression that she was eating, but almost none of it made its way to her mouth. When, at her parents' insistence, she joined the family for a trip to their favorite ice cream parlor, she asked for her strawberry sundae to be boxed to go so she could take it home with her.

"It will melt!" her mother objected. "Why can't you eat it here?"

"I like soupy ice cream," Andi said. "I'll have it as a bedtime snack. I'm sure I'll be hungry by then."

But she didn't wait around long enough to get hungry. Instead, she went up to bed as soon as they got home.

"I don't know why," she said, "but I'm really sleepy."

Now it was Mrs. Walker's turn to regard her daughter with amazement.

"I hope you're not coming down with something," she said worriedly. "This isn't like you, honey. Aren't you feeling well?"

"I'm fine," Andi said. "I'm just tired from all the excitement. It isn't every day that a writer wins a certificate."

She smiled the big awful smile that was so obviously fake that Bruce couldn't imagine how their parents could be taken in by it. His sister might be a good writer, but she was not a good actor.

On his way down the hall to his own room a couple of hours later, Bruce heard a disturbing noise from behind Andi's door. Andi kept her bedroom door closed because she slept with her dog. The children weren't allowed to have their dogs in their bedrooms, but Andi hid Bebe in her closet until after her mother came in to kiss her good night, and then let her out and took her to bed with her.

Mrs. Walker thought Bebe slept in the laundry room.

So now, when Bruce rapped on the door, he was quick to identify himself.

"It's only me," he called softly. "Can I come in?"

"I'm asleep," Andi called back.

"If you were asleep, you wouldn't have heard me," Bruce said. He went in and quickly shoved the door closed behind him. "What was that noise I just heard? It sounded like somebody choking. Was Mom right about you being sick?"

"Bebe threw up," Andi said. "Strawberries don't seem to agree with her."

"You fed Bebe your strawberry sundae!" Bruce exclaimed in horror. He switched on the overhead light, but when he saw what Bebe had done, he quickly switched it off again. "What were you thinking? You know a dog can't digest a whole strawberry sundae."

"I couldn't stand to waste something so good," Andi said. "I tried to eat it myself, but I couldn't make it go down. I thought Bebe would enjoy it, and she *did* — at least, for a couple of minutes."

At any other time, Bruce would have told her how dumb that was. Andi knew as well as he did that dogs should not be fed certain kinds of people food. But he couldn't bring himself to say anything that would make her feel worse than she already did, because while the light had been on, he had seen her face. Her eyes were red, and her cheeks were puffy and tear-streaked.

"You've been crying," he said, a bit shaken. Andi seldom cried.

"I have *not* been crying," Andi shot back defensively. She paused and then admitted reluctantly, "Well, maybe a little bit. But please don't say anything to Mom. I don't want her coming in here and finding Bebe."

"I don't understand why you're taking this so hard," Bruce said. "You ought to be proud of yourself. Second place is great."

"But it's not good *enough*!" Andi said. "I worked all summer writing *Bobby Strikes Back*, and Jerry probably whipped his book out in two weeks while he was grounded. How could he do that and make it better than my book? I wrote mine over and over, trying to make it perfect. I was thinking that you could take pictures for illustrations. There are so many dogs in our neighborhood, you'd have plenty of models, and your name would be on the book jacket right under mine."

"That would have been cool," Bruce admitted, touched by her thoughtfulness.

"And then there's Aunt Alice," Andi said. "This was going to be for *her*!"

"What does Aunt Alice have to do with this?" Bruce asked in bewilderment.

"I based my hero, Bobby the Basset, on Aunt Alice," Andi told him. "In my story, Bobby proved that old dogs can be smarter and braver than young dogs and that young dogs should listen to them and take them seriously. Bobby saved the dognapped victims in my story, like Aunt Alice helped save the real dognapped victims last summer. I was going to dedicate *Bobby Strikes Back* to her. Now all I'll have to show her is a dumb certificate that probably doesn't even have my name right. The editor addressed her letter to 'Amanda Wallace.'"

"Where is the letter?" Bruce asked.

"On my desk," Andi said. "Tomorrow I'm going to tear it up and flush it down the toilet."

"I'm going to turn the light back on," Bruce said, "and you're going to clean up that mess. I might forget that it's there, and I don't want to step in it."

"I was waiting until Bebe fell asleep to do that," Andi said. "I didn't want to embarrass her."

"Dachshunds are nearsighted," Bruce said. "If she's on your bed, she won't see what you're doing even if she's still awake."

He turned on the light and averted his eyes from the frothy pink puddle on the floor as Andi went into the closet and got the towel that Bebe always sat on when she was in hiding. As Bruce had suspected, Bebe was in Andi's bed, a sausage-shaped lump beneath the blanket. The only part of her sticking out was her nose.

While Andi took care of the cleanup, Bruce went over to her desk and picked up the letter.

Dear Ms. Amanda Wallace,

We are pleased to inform you that your delightful manuscript, Bobby Strikes Back, *has placed second in our Young Author Dog Lovers Contest. Your certificate of merit will be mailed to you in a separate envelope along with your manuscript, which you are now free to enter in other competitions. Next spring we will send you a complimentary copy of the book* Ruffy Dean Joins the Circus *by first-place winner Jerry Gordon, who, coincidentally, also happens to live in Elmwood.*

We hope you will consider entering next year's contest, which will be for Young Author Cat Lovers.

Sincerely,

Jo Ann Bayse, Senior Editor

Pet Lovers Press

"You'll have other chances to get your book published," Bruce said. "It says right here you can enter it in other contests."

"There aren't any other contests like this one," Andi said. Her voice was quivering, and Bruce was afraid she was going to cry again.

He said, "Look, Andi, this isn't the end of the world. Think of all the kids who entered and didn't place at all. Most of them aren't even going to get certificates."

"But think of the one who *will* get his book published!" Andi wailed. "I wouldn't feel nearly as bad having somebody else win if that person felt the way we do about dogs. But after all the horrible things Jerry's done to Red Rover, he shouldn't have been allowed to enter! Even if he's a good writer, and I guess he must be or he wouldn't have won, he doesn't deserve to be known all over the world as a boy who loves dogs!"

Bruce couldn't help agreeing with her. Red Rover had permanent scars on his neck from the rope Jerry had used to harness him to a wagon. Bruce was also furious that the only punishment Jerry had received for the misery he had caused many people the past summer was being grounded for two weeks. Staying in his basement bedroom with its big-screen TV and pool table and computer and huge collection of DVDs could hardly be considered a major punishment.

Bruce tried to think of something to say to make Andi feel better.

"Maybe the publishing house will burn down," he suggested. "Then they won't be able to publish Jerry's book."

But a thought that was more realistic occurred to him.

When they didn't know what to do next, there was always Aunt Alice.

Perhaps she could think of a way to get Andi's book published.

CHAPTER THREE

LOCAL PRODIGY WINS NATIONAL WRITING AWARD

Jerry Gordon, 14, has received a very big piece of good news. Jerry's novel, *Ruffy Dean Joins the Circus*, was awarded first prize in the Young Author Dog Lovers Contest, sponsored by Pet Lovers Press, for a book about dogs written by an author under the age of 16.

Jerry's book will be published in the spring of next year.

"I learned about the contest from a flier in the library," Jerry said. "I spent a lot of time in the library last summer. I love dogs, and I've always dreamed of being a writer, so I knew right away that this was the contest for me."

Jerry said his story is about a mischievous dog named Ruffy who performs in a traveling circus.

"Ruffy has lots of adventures and ends up in a happy home," Jerry said.

Amanda Wallace, 11, also of Elmwood, placed second in the contest.

Beneath the article was a picture of Jerry holding his congratulatory letter from Pet Lovers Press. His shiny blond hair formed a halo around his face. He looked adorable.

"They got Andi's name wrong!" Mr. Walker exclaimed indignantly as the paper was passed from hand to hand at the breakfast table. "I'm going to call the editor and demand a correction."

"Please don't bother," Andi said. "It doesn't matter."

Her voice was flat and unemotional. Bruce thought she sounded like a talking robot. He'd felt more comfortable with her the night before when she was raging and weeping. At least then she'd seemed *human*.

"But you deserve recognition," Mr. Walker

protested. "Your picture should be in the paper right along with Jerry's."

"It's all right, really," Andi said. "I'd hate to be photographed with Jerry. People might think we were friends. May I be excused? I've got homework to do."

"But it's Saturday morning!" Mrs. Walker exclaimed. "You have the whole weekend to do homework. Aren't you and Debbie going to take your dogs to the park?"

Andi and her best friend, Debbie Austin, always took Andi's dog, Bebe, and Debbie's dog, Lola, to the Doggie Park on Saturday mornings so they could play with other dogs. Back when Debbie had written a gossip column for *The Bow-Wow News*, she had gotten her most interesting material by eavesdropping on the conversations of dog owners, who sat on benches and chatted while their dogs were romping.

"Bebe doesn't feel well this morning," Andi said. "She seems to have an upset stomach."

She got up from the table and went upstairs to her room. Even from the kitchen, the family could hear her door slam.

"I'm worried about Andi," Mrs. Walker said. "Something doesn't seem right. Maybe I ought to take her to the doctor for a checkup."

"She'll snap out of it," Bruce told his mother reassuringly. But he wasn't sure he believed that. Andi seemed to have morphed into a total stranger. He felt as if he were watching his vibrant sister transform herself, right before his eyes, into a paper doll that had been left out in the rain.

It was Bruce's habit to take Red running on weekend mornings, so his parents didn't question him about where he was going when he left the breakfast table and went out into the backyard. But when Red came bounding to greet him, he apologetically told the excited dog, "I'm sorry, old boy. We'll have to run later. First I have business to take care of."

Bruce spent a few minutes stroking Red's silky head and scratching behind his floppy ears, and then, to Red's huge disappointment, Bruce left him behind and headed for his great-aunt's house at the end of the block. He couldn't take Red with him to visit Aunt Alice because she was terribly allergic to dogs.

Jerry Gordon was in his driveway, oiling the

wheels of his skateboard. Bruce had to walk right past him.

"Hey, shrimp!" Jerry called out.

"Hey yourself," Bruce said, trying not to show how much he hated that nickname. His parents kept predicting that he would soon have a growth spurt, but they had been promising that for years and it still hadn't happened.

"Did you see the morning paper?" Jerry asked with a smirk.

"I looked at the sports page," Bruce said. "That was all that was worth reading."

"Then you missed the big news," Jerry told him. "I made front-page headlines! I've written a book and it's going to be published! I'm already getting phone calls from TV producers who saw my picture in the paper and want me to be on talk shows."

"I just bet!" Bruce said sarcastically, but he had a sneaking suspicion that it might be true. Jerry probably could do a great interview with someone like Oprah. Any boy who was glib enough to talk the police out of arresting him on dognapping charges could charm his way into the hearts of television viewers.

Quickening his pace, Bruce continued past the

Gordons' house and turned up the neatly paved walkway to the house next door. He rang the bell and waited patiently for Aunt Alice to respond. His father's elderly aunt was not an early riser, and her joints could be stiff in the mornings, which meant it might take her a while to get to the door. But she always got there eventually and did so now, peering through the peephole to identify her visitor. Aunt Alice did not open her door to people who sold magazine subscriptions.

She hadn't yet dressed for the day and was still in her pink flowered housecoat, but her face lit up with pleasure when she saw who her caller was.

"My gracious, it's chilly!" she exclaimed as the brisk morning air swept in through the open door-way. "Hurry, dear, and come in! Spring apparently hasn't sprung yet, though my hyacinths don't know the difference. The purple ones are already popping their heads up. I suppose you're here to discuss that article in the paper?"

"So you've already seen it?" Bruce asked.

"How could I have missed it when my next-door neighbors' son is all over the front page?" Aunt Alice led the way into her immaculate white-carpeted living room, where no cushion was ever out of place on the lemon yellow sofa. Bruce was suddenly aware that he was wearing the same jeans he'd worn for most of the past week. He decided that it might be best if he didn't sit down.

The morning paper was spread across Aunt Alice's coffee table, and Jerry smiled sweetly up at them from the center of a round wet circle where Aunt Alice had set her coffee cup on his face.

"How is Andi reacting to this?" she asked Bruce. "I haven't read *Bobby Strikes Back*, but she's told me about it. A lot of her heart went into writing that story."

"She's putting on a good act," Bruce said. "But that's all it is — an act. Mom and Dad are buying it, but I know she's faking. Last night she was crying in her bedroom and looked just awful. She expected to win that contest. She was totally *sure*."

"She must be devastated," Aunt Alice said sympathetically. "Not because she came in second — although losing to Jerry must have been a bitter pill to swallow — but because she was living for a dream and now she doesn't have one. People as driven as Andi can't function without a dream. They have to have something to strive for or they lose their energy."

"Is that normal?" Bruce asked. He planned to be a photojournalist, but that was a goal for the future. For now, he was happy just to have fun taking pictures and running with his dog and hanging out with Tim and his other friends. It had never occurred to him to submit his photographs to magazines, which Andi had been doing with her poetry since she was ten.

"It's not normal for everyone, but it's normal for Andi," Aunt Alice said. "Andi isn't your average young girl. That makes her life more interesting but also more difficult. Do the rules allow her to enter her manuscript in other contests?"

"The publisher said she could," Bruce answered. "But there aren't many contests for kids who write books about dogs."

"There don't have to be many," Aunt Alice said. "There just needs to be one. Since Andi is too dejected right now to pursue this on her own, it's up to the people who love her to do that for her. Let's go online and see what we can come up with."

She led the way up the stairs and down the hall to her home office, which once had been a sewing room but now was devoted to legal and investigative materials. When Aunt Alice's husband, Peter, had been alive, the two of them had run a detective agency. That had been a long time ago, and in the years since her husband's death, Aunt Alice had devoted herself to charitable causes and gardening. However, she had recently purchased a computer and become intrigued by the new technology she'd read about on the Internet. She had been ordering books about forensics and DNA evidence and new methods for running background checks on suspicious people. She had even started talking about renewing her private detective's license.

Now she switched on her computer, pulled up her favorite search engine, and typed in the words "Dogs + writing + contest." To Bruce's surprise, a page popped up with links to a variety of Web sites, but none of the contests seemed right for Andi's novel. Almost all were sponsored by dog food companies that wanted jingles to use in their commercials. The prizes were cans of dog food.

Aunt Alice went back to the search engine and substituted the word "story" for the word "writing." This time, when she hit ENTER, the list was shorter, and there still didn't seem to be any contests for books.

"Andi was right," Bruce said. "Pet Lovers Press was a onetime chance for her. They're the only publisher looking for books by kids who write about animals, and it seems as if they're going to keep switching subjects. Their next contest is going to be about cats, and then they'll probably do hamsters and horses and goldfish. By the time they get back to dogs again, Andi will be too old to enter."

"We mustn't give up hope," Aunt Alice said, scrolling down the page. "Here's one that looks interesting. It isn't specifically for children, but it doesn't exclude them either. Your parents gave you a video camera for Christmas. I assume you've been learning to use it. Have you mastered your craft yet?"

"I'm pretty good," Bruce told her. "I'm taking a video class as my eighth-grade elective and learning about editing and sound tracks and stuff like that."

He leaned in closer so he could read over her shoulder.

STAR BURST STUDIOS' DOGS IN ACTION VIDEO CONTEST! Every dog has a story, and your pup pal is no exception. You may be the owner of the next canine superstar! Send us a fifteen-minute video based on the most dramatic event in the life of your family pooch, and maybe your talented tail-wagger will make it to Hollywood! The three top videos will be aired on national television, and the winner will be decided by votes from our viewers. The dog who stars in the winning video will be offered the opportunity to appear in commercials and movies produced by professional filmmakers. Entry must be accompanied by a signed consent form for each person who appears and/or is heard in the video submission. Only one entry per person or group will be accepted, and all entries must be received by April 30. The finalists will be announced on May 14.

"I'll print a copy of the entry form," Aunt Alice said. "You'll have to work fast to meet this deadline, but this sounds to me like a *Bobby Strikes Back* type of contest. Even though Andi changed some of the names and details, her story is based on a true event in Red Rover's life."

"But it's a contest for a video, not for a book," Bruce said doubtfully.

"Then Andi must turn her story into a screenplay," said Aunt Alice.

CHAPTER FOUR

"A video is *not* better than a book!" Andi protested. "*Nothing* is better than a book! You can hold a book in your hands and smell the pages and read it in the bathtub!"

"Is that why you hog the bathroom for hours?" Bruce asked her. "How do you soap yourself if you're busy sniffing pages?" He had expected Andi to be thrilled with this new proposal, and here she was, griping about it before they'd even discussed it. "It's the story that matters, isn't it? You want people to know about Bobby, and this way they won't just read about him, they'll see him. And *dogs* will see him. Dogs can't read, but they can watch DVDs. You know how much Bully Bernstein enjoys movies."

Andi nodded, brightening a little. She would never forget her first glimpse of that overweight bulldog sprawled on the sofa in the Bernsteins' living room, watching *Lady and the Tramp*. Bully had been the subject of the lead story in the first edition of *The Bow-Wow News*.

"I guess you're right," she said. "Dogs probably would like a video. But how will we film it and where will we get the actors?"

"My video camera will be perfect for this," Bruce said. "I can do the editing in the photo lab at school. Tell me the plot of your book. How large a cast will we need?"

"Well, there's Bobby, the old basset hound," Andi began. "He's in love with Juliet, the poodle who lives next door. Bobby can't visit her, because her cruel owner, Mr. Rinkle, has put up a big iron wall between the houses. One day Bobby gets out of his yard and runs down the alley and tries to get into Juliet's yard. Mr. Rinkle catches him and throws him in his toolshed. Then Mr. Rinkle decides he enjoys dognapping, and he dognaps all the dogs in the neighborhood and stuffs them in with Bobby."

"That's a lot of action," Bruce said, beginning to feel excited. "I could get some dramatic footage of Mr. Rinkle grabbing the dogs. How does the story end?"

"Bobby convinces the dogs to work as a team," Andi said. "They climb on top of each other to form

a pyramid with Bobby at the top. Then, all together, when Bobby gives the command, they take a big breath and swell up like balloons and push Bobby up through the roof. He pops out and frees the other dogs, and they all run home."

"Great!" Bruce said. "This should be a cinch to film. We won't need any human actors except Mr. Rinkle, and we know a lot of dogs we can use as extras. We can film it in our backyard. We don't have a wall or a toolshed, but we do have a chain-link fence, and Tim and I can build a shed."

"Tim!" Andi exclaimed. "Why does Tim have to be involved in this? This is our movie — yours and mine! It's not like the newspaper, where we needed Tim to be the publisher."

"I need him to help me build the shed," Bruce said. "Tim's got the tools and scrap lumber. Besides, he's better at things like that than I am. We'll need to get the shed built fast so we can do the filming next weekend. We've got a very tight deadline."

"If you're bringing in Tim, then I'm bringing in Debbie," Andi said. "It isn't fair to include your best friend and not mine."

"We don't need Debbie," Bruce objected. "Debbie's a ding-a-ling. There's nothing for her to

do except distract you. You've got to write the film script while Tim and I build the shed."

"Debbie can be a part of the cast," Andi said. "She can play the role of one of the dog owners. In fact, she can be *all* the owners! She can wear disguises and first be the owner of one dog and then of another, and grieve and cry because she can't afford to pay the ransom. I can't wait to get started! I'm certain we can win this contest!"

The zombie-like girl from the breakfast table had vanished as quickly as she had materialized. Andi's eyes were sparkling and she was on fire with enthusiasm. Bruce realized that Aunt Alice had been right. All Andi had needed to bring her back to life was a new challenge.

"Okay," he said, giving in because he didn't want to argue with her. "Debbie can grieve for the victims and be our casting director. That will keep her out of our hair while you're writing the script."

Constructing the toolshed turned out to be less of a problem than Bruce had anticipated, because Tim suggested that they build only the front of the shed.

"That's how they do it in Hollywood," he said as the boys lugged the lumber from Tim's side yard across the street and down the alley to the Walkers'

backyard. "In movies, when they show a row of houses, they're usually not real. They're just fake fronts, called facades. We'll build a facade that looks like the front of a toolshed. When Mr. Rinkle shoves the dogs through the door, they'll come right out the back. Then one of us can grab them and bring them around to the front so Mr. Rinkle can stuff them through again. He'll have an endless supply of victims."

"What about when Bobby bursts through the roof?" Bruce asked. "If we use a facade, there'll be nothing to support a rooftop."

"We won't need to actually show the rooftop," Tim said. "You can film the facade straight on but from a low angle, and the girls and I will be hiding behind it. When you're ready for Bobby to appear, we'll give him a boost. His head will suddenly pop out over the top of the facade, and it will look like he's come through the roof, even though there isn't one. By the way, who's going to play the part of Bobby? The only basset I know about is Delaney Belanger's dog, and the last time I saw him, he had mange and his hair was falling out."

"We'll change the basset to an Irish setter," Bruce said. "That way we can use Red."

"Andi won't go for that," Tim told him with certainty. He'd come to know his friend's stubborn sister all too well when they'd worked together on the newspaper. "She'll throw a fit if we don't stick exactly to her story line."

"She'll have to go along with it," Bruce said. "She won't have a choice. We don't have a basset, so we're going to have to use Red. In real life Red did get dognapped along with a bunch of other dogs. In her book Andi made him a basset, so now she can change him back again."

Andi and Debbie were seated at the kitchen table, preparing a list of dogs to invite to be cast members, when Bruce, with Tim trailing reluctantly behind him, announced his decision that Red was going to be Bobby.

Tim's prediction was accurate. Andi was outraged.

"In my story Bobby is a basset — a *basset*!" she said vehemently. "Bruce, I told you that Bobby's a basset! Let's run an ad in the paper and see if we can find one."

"We can't afford to run ads in the paper," Bruce told her. "Besides, people who answer an ad would expect their bassets to be paid, and we don't have the money to do that. And the rules of the contest say this has to be based on *our* dog's story. The star of the video has to belong to us."

"But Bobby is supposed to be old!" Andi argued. "That's the whole point of my story. Red's shiny and young-looking. He doesn't fit the part."

"We can sprinkle him with cornstarch," Bruce said. "That will make him gray."

"We could do the same thing with Bebe," Andi said as a new idea occurred to her. "If Bobby can't be a basset, then I want him to be a dachshund. Bebe belongs to us just as much as Red does. Why shouldn't *she* win a chance to go to Hollywood and be famous?"

"Bebe looks like a long fat worm," Bruce said. "Bebe is not star material."

"She is!" Andi cried. "She's brilliant and sensitive and talented!"

Debbie said, "I'm the casting director, and I'm casting Bebe."

When Andi had insisted on Debbie's being part of the project, Bruce had been afraid that exactly this sort of thing would happen. No matter what outrageous idea his sister came up with, Debbie would leap to her support.

"There's no way that Bebe can play that part," he

said firmly. "Bobby has to unlatch the gate to get out of his yard. He'll also have to unlatch the door to the toolshed to let the other dogs escape. Bebe doesn't know how to do that."

"She can learn!" Andi said. "I can teach her!"

"There isn't time to train her," Bruce said. "It took me a month to teach Red Rover that trick. Besides, a dachshund's too low to the ground to reach the latch. She'd hurt her back if she tried."

"Oh, all right," Andi said ungraciously. "I suppose it will have to be Red. But I want you to get a lot of close-ups of Bebe so talent scouts will be enchanted by her. If Red goes to Hollywood, I want her to go, too."

"What about Bobby's girlfriend, Juliet?" Debbie asked them. "The rules don't say that you have to own the costar. Maybe we could use my dog, Lola. A Chinese crested hairless is so exotic."

Lola wasn't really a Chinese crested hairless, but Debbie kept her shaved so she looked like one.

"In my story, Juliet is a poodle," Andi said. "I want to stick to the story as much as possible. We do know a poodle — Snowflake Swanson. She can be Bobby's sweetheart."

"Do you think Mrs. Swanson will agree to that?" Tim asked doubtfully. "After all, Snowflake is a show dog. Mrs. Swanson might want to charge us for using her."

"Snowflake is a has-been," Debbie said. "When I was doing undercover work for the gossip column, I learned that Snowflake hasn't placed in a dog show in years. Mrs. Swanson should be thrilled for Snowflake to be in a movie. Lots of washed-up beauty queens become actresses."

"Who will we get to play Mr. Rinkle?" Tim asked. It was the question they all had been avoiding. "It'll have to be one of our dads, but not mine. He's so shy he won't even play charades."

"Mine won't do it either," Debbie said. "We'll need to film on a weekend, and he'd never give up his golf games. So that just leaves Mr. Walker. What do you think, Bruce?"

"It's worth a shot," Bruce said. "But we hardly see our dad on weekends. He's always working, even if it's at home at his computer."

"I'm sure we can talk him into it," Andi said. "He won't need to learn a lot of lines. All he'll have to do is say, 'Ha, ha, ha.'"

However, when they approached him, Mr. Walker

told them regretfully that although he was eager to encourage them in their creative projects, he wouldn't be available on the coming weekend.

"I'm going to have to spend both Saturday and Sunday preparing a report for an important meeting," he said. "If you're willing to wait until the next weekend, it's possible I might be able to find some time then."

"This can't wait," Bruce told him. "The deadline for submissions is April thirtieth, and I'll have to get in line to use the editing bay at school. If we don't do the filming next weekend, we might as well bag it. Our video won't be finished in time."

"We *have* to enter it!" Andi cried. "I've already told Bebe about it. She's all excited!"

They sat silent for a moment, contemplating possibilities.

Then their eyes met, and they nodded simultaneously.

"We have to use the weapon at hand," Bruce said. "Since the iron wall in your story is now a chain-link fence, and your basset is now an Irish setter, is there any reason why the villain can't be *Mrs. Rinkle?*"

CHAPTER FIVE

"How close would I have to get to the dogs?" Aunt Alice asked. "Would I have to touch them?"

"Yes," Bruce admitted. "But you wouldn't have to cuddle them. You'd just scoop them up and shove them through a door. You could wear long sleeves and gloves and maybe a face mask. You know those pollen masks they advertise on television?"

"I've seen those ads," Aunt Alice said. "I suppose it might do the job. Especially if I take an allergy pill beforehand and hold the dogs down low, away from my face."

"It's a very low door," Bruce assured her. "Once you get the dogs down to that level, you can shove them through with your knees."

"That might work," Aunt Alice acknowledged. "I do want to participate in this worthy endeavor.

After all, I'm the one who suggested it. When will you need me on the set?"

"Next Saturday," Bruce said. "We'll do all the big scenes then, including the ones that you're in. We'll film some minor scenes during the week, after school, in order to get a head start. Like the one where Bobby is sitting by the fence, dreaming about Juliet. And the scenes where Debbie is grieving. You won't need to be there for those."

"But won't you be getting the scenes out of order?" Aunt Alice asked him. "Don't I have to snatch the dogs before Debbie starts grieving?"

"In the story, yes, but not in the filming," Bruce explained. "I can film the scenes in any order I want and rearrange them during editing. Then we're going to have to make an audiotape of Andi reading the story so viewers will understand what the dogs are thinking. There's a lot of technical stuff involved in filmmaking."

The production schedule was complicated by their having to spend so much of each weekday at school. On Tuesday, Andi faked a stomachache so she could stay home and work all day on the script. Because Mr. and Mrs. Walker were both at work, she didn't have to lie in bed and act sick, and was able to accomplish a lot. However, all four children could not claim stomachaches simultaneously without arousing suspicion, so they tried to cram as much activity as possible into the few precious hours between when school let out and when they were expected home for dinner.

In those after-school hours, Bruce and Tim constructed the toolshed and Debbie canvassed the neighborhood for dog actors. By Wednesday, she was able to report proudly that she had assembled a cast of eight in addition to Red Rover and Bebe.

Mrs. Swanson had happily agreed to Snowflake's playing the part of Juliet and had even volunteered to take her to the beauty parlor to get her hair done and her toenails painted for the occasion.

"This will do wonders for Snowflake's self-esteem," Mrs. Swanson said. "The poor dear has been so depressed since she stopped winning ribbons. The idea of starring in a movie is bound to rejuvenate her."

Debbie didn't have the heart to tell her that Snowflake's role was a minor one. All she had to do was look glamorous.

Debbie had also enlisted Trixie, Foxy, Curly, Fifi, and Frisky from the Doggie Park, along with her own dog, Lola, and Tim's dog, MacTavish.

The Bernsteins regretfully declined to let Bully participate, because Saturday was his birthday and they were having a party for him.

"I understand," Debbie told them. "We'll miss Bully terribly, but I hope he gets lots of presents."

Secretly she was relieved that they wouldn't have to worry about Aunt Alice straining her knees as she attempted to cram the massive bulldog through the door of the toolshed.

On Thursday, they filmed three scenes in which Debbie was grieving. In one she wore a scarf; in another, a baseball cap; and in the third, one of her mother's hair extensions. She looked like a different person in each of the shots.

Bruce thought the performance was ridiculous, but Andi had written the scenes especially for Debbie and was insistent that they be included.

"Those scenes provide drama," she said. "They're very important."

On Friday, they filmed Bobby gazing wistfully out through the chain-link fence, hoping for a glimpse of Juliet. Bruce got that scene in one take, because Red was perfect. The talcum powder had turned him gray enough to satisfy even Andi, and when Bruce went out into the alley with his camera, Red, who had expected to be taken for a run, gazed through the fence with an expression of such longing that it would have broken the heart of anyone who'd seen it. Then Bruce went back into the yard and shot the scene in which Bobby opened the gate and ran into the alley. That, too, was done in one take. As soon as Bruce shouted, "Open, sesame!" Red rushed to the gate, took the latch in his mouth, and shoved the gate open.

"How did you teach him to do that?" Tim asked in amazement.

"It's a step-by-step process," Bruce explained. "First you teach your dog to go to the gate. Then you teach him the command 'paws up.' Then you smear chopped liver on the latch, and while he's licking it off, you yell, 'Open, sesame!' and help him push the gate open. After a while he learns to put all those steps together and does the whole thing on his own whenever you tell him to."

"Awesome!" Tim said. "I'm going to teach MacTavish to open the freezer and bring me a dish of ice cream. What's next on our shooting agenda?"

"I could grieve again!" Debbie offered eagerly. "I haven't grieved for Trixie yet."

"We've got more than enough shots of you grieving," Bruce said. "What we need now is some action. Let's film the scene where Red pops up through the roof."

A voice spoke suddenly from behind them.

"What are you guys doing?"

Jerry Gordon was standing in the alley, peering at them over the gate.

"What does it look like I'm doing?" Bruce responded irritably. "I'm taking pictures of my dog."

"The dog you bought with dirty money," Jerry said. "The money you made from that newspaper with all those fake articles. I heard about how Mr. Murdock was threatening to sue you."

"We didn't print any fake articles," Andi said defensively. "We just printed an article with a photo Mr. Murdock didn't like. Bruce bought Red from your father fair and square with money we earned before Mr. Murdock got mad at us."

"Red is your brother's dog in name only," Jerry told her. "I was Red's first master and he'll never forget that. All I have to do is raise my hand and he'll obey me. Watch this!"

With his eyes glued to Red's, he lifted his hand and made a fist.

The big dog began to tremble, and before Bruce could do anything to calm him, he leapt to his feet and raced frantically to take shelter in his doghouse.

"Sure he remembers you!" Bruce said angrily. "He's scared to death of you! Get out of here, Jerry. We're busy, and you're messing up our schedule."

"You can't tell me to get out of this alley," Jerry said. "The alley is public property. Anybody can stand here." Now that Red was no longer there for him to torment, he turned his attention to the toolshed facade. "What's that big piece of plywood with a door in it? When I saw you dragging those boards down the alley to your place, I thought you were going to build a clubhouse. But that thing isn't any clubhouse. What the heck is it?"

"That's none of your business," Andi told him. "Go away and let us get on with what we're doing."

"We can't get on with it even if he leaves," Bruce said in frustration, snapping the lens cap back onto his camera. "He's got Red spooked. He's too scared to come out of his doghouse."

"Then that's it for today," Tim said. "It's no big deal, Bruce. We'd have to quit soon anyway, because the light's starting to fade. We'll film the roof-busting scene tomorrow after Red's calmed down. Jerry, feel free to stand in the alley all night. It doesn't matter to us."

"That's okay," Jerry said. "I'll come back in the morning. I wouldn't miss the 'roof-busting scene' for anything. Maybe I'll come on my skateboard. I know how much Red enjoys seeing me on that."

He turned and casually strolled off with his hands in his pockets. Anyone watching would have thought that he had been paying them a friendly visit.

"He *will* be back tomorrow," Andi said miserably after Jerry was out of earshot. "He'll spook Red again and wreck the big scene with Mrs. Rinkle. Red will never perform if Jerry is standing there, giving him the evil eye."

"That's not going to happen," Tim said. "Bruce and I will rearrange the set. We'll rotate the facade so it's facing the other direction and blocks Red's view of the alley."

"That might work for the dog-stuffing scene, but not for the roof-busting scene," Bruce said. "Once you and the girls boost Red up so his head sticks over the facade, he'll be able to see in all directions."

"We'll get up at dawn to shoot that scene," Tim said. "Jerry won't get here that early. By the time he does, the roof-busting scene will be a wrap, and on top of that, he'll have your Aunt Alice to deal with."

CHAPTER SIX

"You mean all I get to say is 'ha, ha, ha'?" Aunt Alice asked incredulously. "That's my only line in the whole movie?"

As Bruce had suggested, she was wearing her gardening gloves and a long-sleeved blouse to prevent her from having more contact than necessary with dog hair. She was also wearing a pollen mask, which was nothing at all like the wispy white masks shown in television ads. This one was huge and black, and it covered the entire lower half of her face. She looked like an invader from outer space.

"That's the dialogue I put in the script," Andi said, referring to her sheaf of papers. "'Mrs. Rinkle hauls Bobby over to the toolshed and shoves him in on top of the lawn mower. Mrs. Rinkle (laughing wickedly): Ha, ha, ha!'"

"And for that I went to all the effort of carving a hole in this mask so I could talk?" Aunt Alice said. "What a waste of energy! Please tell me I'm permitted to ad-lib."

"Of course," Andi said, because Aunt Alice was obviously disappointed. "Say whatever you feel in your heart when you see those dogs' pitiful faces. I'm sure it will be perfect."

Andi was so relieved that Tim's plan to shoot the roof-busting scene at sunrise had been successful that she would have agreed happily to anything. Shooting at dawn had proved to be an inspiration. Seeing Red Rover's beautiful head, framed by the orange globe of the early-morning sun, rise majestically over the top of the toolshed had been an unforgettable experience.

"The first dog you shove through the door of the shed will be Bobby," Andi now explained to Aunt Alice. "That won't be a problem, because Red does whatever Bruce tells him. You'll barely have to touch him, and he'll race in that door."

"Are you ready, Bruce?" asked Aunt Alice.

"Let's do it!" Bruce said. He turned to his dog and commanded, "Red, door — *go!*"

Red dashed to the toolshed so fast that Aunt Alice had to leap to pretend to grab hold of him before he went in.

"That was easy," she said, panting a little from the exertion. "Who's next?"

"The next one is Lola," Andi said, consulting her script. "This will be easy, too, since you already know her. It won't be like grabbing a stranger."

"Lights! Camera! Action!" Aunt Alice cried before Bruce could open his mouth. "*Ha, ha, ha!*"

She snatched up Lola and, holding her as far from her face as possible, began to berate her. "Ha, ha, ha, you pitiful excuse for an animal! This will teach your irresponsible owners to leave you unguarded when dog-hating Mrs. Rinkle is in the neighborhood! *Ha, ha, HA!*"

Her voice rose to a shriek as she thrust poor Lola through the door.

Debbie, who was waiting behind the facade to receive the dogs as they came through, snatched Lola up in her arms and cuddled her close.

"Mrs. Scudder, you scared Lola to death!" she cried accusingly. "How could you frighten her like that? She's always thought you liked her!"

"I do like her," Aunt Alice said in her normal

voice. "I became quite fond of sweet little Lola when we used her as bait to catch the Gordon boys in their crime spree. But, Debbie, dear, movies aren't real. I'm playing the part of someone very different from myself. If Lola wants to be an actress, she must get used to that concept."

Bruce, who had turned off his camera when Debbie's voice had cut into the scene, stared at Aunt Alice in astonishment.

"How did you do that?" he asked. "You turned yourself into an ogre!"

"You were incredible!" Andi regarded her great-aunt with awe. "Where did you learn to be an actor?"

"It was back when I was a private detective," Aunt Alice told her. "Part of my job was pretending to be different people. Sometimes I would sit all evening in a nightclub, sipping a cocktail, listening to conversation at the next table. Of course, I drank only soda, because I had to stay sharp and alert, but I got a lot of valuable information that way. Sometimes I'd dress in work clothes and pretend to be a janitor in an office building and eavesdrop on financial discussions. Each assignment was different."

"You're a pro!" Andi exclaimed in delight. "This movie is going to be wonderful!"

Aunt Alice sneezed.

"Maybe not," she said. "I probably shouldn't have cut a hole in the mask, because the dander from the dog hair is starting to leak in. I'm going to sneeze again — I feel it coming — *At-choo!*"

"Oh, no!" Debbie cried. "And you only just barely touched Lola, who has hardly any hair at all. What's going to happen when you have to handle the others — Trixie and Frisky and Curly — especially Curly! Curly's owner never bathes him. Even I sneeze when I'm around Curly!"

"Then, by all means, let's skip Curly," Aunt Alice said. "Not to fear, my dears, I shall soldier through. However, I'm afraid that I'm going to keep on sneezing. Is there a way you can work my sneezing into your script?"

They all looked expectantly at Andi.

"I've changed the story so much already, I guess I can put in some sneezes," Andi said thoughtfully. "I'll rewrite it to say that Mrs. Rinkle isn't dog-napping because she's evil; she's doing it for the sake of her health. The neighborhood's filled with dogs, and Mrs. Rinkle is so allergic to them that she's sneezing herself to death. So she decides to collect them all and stuff them into her toolshed."

"But then she'll have to pack up and move," Debbie said. "She can't continue to live in a house with a shed filled with dogs right there in her backyard."

"That's true," Andi said. "But that makes the story even better. Mrs. Rinkle moves out of the country and abandons the dogs. They're hungry and thirsty. It's a life-and-death situation. That's when Bobby bursts out and frees them. If we're going to skip Curly, the next dog through the door will be Frisky."

Bruce started the camera rolling.

"Now it's your turn, Frisky!" screamed Aunt Alice, grabbing the trembling animal and flexing her knees to shove him through the doorway. *"You obnoxious, fluffy monster! You allergy-activating ball of dander! In you go — At-choo!"*

Bruce had barely finished filming that scene when they heard the whir of skateboard wheels in the alley.

A moment later, Jerry shouted, "Gesundheit! Was that my next-door neighbor, Mrs. Scudder, doing all that sneezing?"

"Jerry?" Aunt Alice turned to glare at the handsome young man who was hanging over the gate and smiling at her angelically. "If I were you, I'd remove myself from these premises. I didn't press assault and battery charges against your cousin, but I filed a report with the police department, and it's not too late for me to initiate a lawsuit."

Jerry just smiled again. "I'll testify for Connor. I'll say you tripped over your own feet, and people will believe me. By the way, I talked to Connor last night. He said to tell all of you hi. He can't wait to come back to Elmwood for another visit."

"First he'll have to get out of the detention center," Bruce said.

"Who said Connor's in jail?" Jerry asked. "None of the dog owners pressed charges. They were too happy to get their pets back. Connor's a senior at a private high school in Chicago and he's doing great. He took the prettiest girl in the school to the senior prom, and they got crowned king and queen. He's already been offered a scholarship to Harvard. Then he's planning to go to law school."

"That doesn't surprise me," Aunt Alice said. "Connor was born to be a politician. He'll be a senator and then he'll probably run for president. But he's not here now, so he can't intercede for you, Jerry, and I command you to step away from that gate. The alley is public property, but that gate is not." She turned back to Bruce. "Now, shall we proceed with the filming? *At-choo — at-choo! Come here, Bebe, you rat-fanged varmint!*"

"Don't traumatize her!" Andi cried, but Aunt Alice had already snatched up Bebe and was shoving her through the door. Bebe was long and slick, so she slid through easily, and Aunt Alice sneezed again and made a grab for Trixie.

Trixie, who had been featured in *The Bow-Wow News* as a "hero dog," was determined to uphold her reputation. She barked and tried to bite Aunt Alice's hand.

"No problem," Aunt Alice assured the children. "My garden gloves are as tough as rawhide. *In you go, Trixie, you jagged-toothed vixen! How dare you attempt to defend yourself against the mighty Mrs. Rinkle?*"

Although the facade they had built blocked Jerry from view, they could hear the sound of his skateboard as he cruised the alley. When Bruce backed off to get a long shot of the toolshed, he could see Jerry's head whizzing past on the far side of the fence, going first in one direction and then the other. He was clearly trying to intimidate Red and the other dogs, but because the dogs couldn't see him, he didn't produce the emotional effect he was hoping for.

It was midday by the time they completed the scenes that involved Mrs. Rinkle. Aunt Alice, obviously weary, but also looking quite pleased with herself, went home to take a well-deserved nap, and Debbie assembled her cast of extras behind the facade for the grand finale.

Red stood in front of the shed, his whole attention focused on Bruce. He seemed to understand the importance of this final scene and was determined to make his master proud of him.

"Open, sesame!" Bruce shouted, and off Red flew.

He bounded to the door of the shed, stood up on his hind feet, and seized the latch in his teeth. The door flew open, and the dogs behind it poured out. The moment they were out of camera range, Tim and Debbie grabbed them and carried them around to the back of the facade to feed them through again.

"What kind of crazy film are you making?" Jerry yelled.

Now that Aunt Alice was gone, he was back at the gate.

At the sound of the hated voice, Red gave a yelp of terror and fled to his doghouse, but for once, Bruce wasn't worried about that reaction. Their day's work was over and he would comfort his dog later.

He turned off his camera and grinned at his sister.

"We got it!" he told her. "This is going to be terrific!"

Bruce could not remember the last time he had hugged Andi. In fact, he couldn't remember *ever* having hugged her. She was his *sister*. Guys didn't *ever* hug their sisters!

But this was a special occasion. He hugged her now.

CHAPTER SEVEN

Bruce was right. It *was* terrific. And he finished it not only on time, but three days before the deadline.

That was largely thanks to his photography teacher, Mr. Talbert, who, upon learning that Bruce was preparing an entry for a contest, allowed him to use the editing bay after school hours, along with a student named Kristy Fernald, who also was working on a personal project. Mr. Talbert even stayed after school to help them shift the order of scenes and make voice-overs coincide with the action.

"It's not often that I have students take on projects of this magnitude," Mr. Talbert said. "Kristy has been working on hers for over a month, and I'm very impressed with her accomplishment."

Bruce glanced at the girl who was using the computer next to his. When he saw the footage she was editing, he couldn't help being surprised. All the people in her video were either bald or gray-haired, and some were in wheelchairs or using walkers. In general, though, they seemed to be having a good time, especially one group who was wearing birthday hats, pointing at something off camera, and laughing uproariously.

"These scenes are from the Glenn Ridge Assisted Living Facility," Kristy said in response to Bruce's unspoken question. "My mom's a physical therapist there. I told the directors I'd make a video they could show to people who are thinking of moving there. The filming was easy, but the editing's taken me forever. I'm hoping to get it finished today."

"That's nice of you," Bruce said. "I'm making a movie to enter in Star Burst Studios' *Dogs in Action* video contest. My great-aunt found it online. The finalists will be on TV and people will vote for the winner."

"The two of you are a credit to our school," Mr. Talbert said. "Just like Jerry Gordon, who won that young authors competition. We have a lot of talented students at Elmwood Middle School."

"In the fall you're going to have another one," Bruce told him. "My sister, Andi, is going to be starting seventh grade. Andi's an awesome writer.

She took second place in that contest Jerry Gordon won, and she wrote her story when she was only eleven."

"Really?" Mr. Talbert seemed surprised. "I read in the paper that the second-place winner was from Elmwood, but I didn't realize she was your sister. I thought the girl's last name was Wallace."

"That was a misprint," Bruce said. "My sister's name is Andrea Walker. I haven't seen Jerry's story, but it's hard to believe that it's any better than Andi's."

Bruce completed what he hoped was the final edit of the video the following afternoon, and that evening he and the others gathered in front of the TV in Aunt Alice's living room for what they referred to as the grand premiere. They considered inviting their parents, but then decided not to, in case there turned out to be problems that needed fixing. Bruce, in particular, was worried that the video would not look as perfect on a TV screen as it had on the computer in the editing bay.

Andi had expected to be excited when the title *Bobby Strikes Back* appeared on the screen, but she had not imagined how intense that emotion would be. She sat, mesmerized, as the credits began to roll and she saw her name appear at the top of the list.

Andrea Walker — Writer and Narrator
Bruce Walker — Photographer and Executive
Producer
Timothy Kelly — Coproducer and Carpenter
Deborah Austin — Casting Director and Griever
Alice Scudder — Mrs. Rinkle

Then Andi's own voice began to recite the story that she had spent so many months writing and rewriting: *"Bobby, the old Irish setter, sat by the chain-link fence, gazing into the alley."* Red appeared on the screen, peering mournfully through the fence, as Andi's narration continued: *"Bobby's next-door neighbor, Mrs. Rinkle, had built an iron wall between their houses, because she didn't want Bobby to see his sweetheart, Juliet. Juliet, who was the only dog Mrs. Rinkle wasn't allergic to, was ravishingly beautiful. Bobby only had a chance of catching a glimpse of her if she escaped from her yard and fled into the alley. So far that had not occurred, but Bobby clung to the hope that someday it might."*

Bruce's camera zoomed in on Snowflake Swanson, newly fluffed from her trip to the beauty parlor, her glamorous purple toenails gleaming in the sunlight. It was obvious why Bobby had fallen in love with her. Any male dog would have been smitten with Juliet, whether or not she was winning ribbons at dog shows.

The dognapping scenes were interesting, because in an effort to lessen Aunt Alice's exposure to the dogs, Bruce had not shown her snatching them. He had filmed the victims romping happily about in their yards, and then, with the help of Mr. Talbert, he had created a special effect that made them suddenly vanish. One moment a yard had a dog in it, and an instant later that dog was gone, as though sucked up by a gigantic vacuum cleaner.

"Wow!" Tim exclaimed. "That's like something out of a sci-fi movie!"

Then the scene abruptly shifted to the Walkers' backyard.

"Oh, my!" Aunt Alice said softly as her black-masked image appeared on-screen. She leaned forward and watched with fascination as her alter ego, Mrs. Rinkle, snatched up little pink-skinned

Lola, who yelped in terror. *"Ha, ha, ha, you pitiful excuse for an animal!"* Aunt Alice mouthed in sync with the woman on the screen. *"Ha, ha, HA!* I wish I had made the hole in the mask bigger so I could have bared my teeth."

"You were perfect!" Andi said. "I don't think your teeth could have made this any scarier. Oh, here's the scene where Debbie is grieving for Lola! Debbie, you're a marvelous griever. Those look like real tears."

"I sliced up an onion and rubbed it on my face," Debbie said. "I cry even harder in the next scene, when I'm grieving for Bebe. See? My eyes are bloodshot and my nose is running. That time I used a red onion. They're stronger than yellow ones."

That scene dissolved, and Aunt Alice appeared with Frisky. *"At-choo!"* She sneezed so hard that she almost blew the mask off.

"Mrs. Rinkle's allergies were making her life miserable," Andi's voice informed viewers. *"She knew she could not survive with a shed filled with dogs. So she left them behind and moved to China, where most of the dogs are hairless."*

"We're missing a part," Debbie said. "Where's

the scene where I grieve for Frisky? That was a good one, because I was wearing Mom's hair extensions. I looked like a Mid-Evil princess."

"I had to cut that scene," Bruce said. "There are restrictions on the length of the video. I needed to save time for the finale. *And here it comes!*"

The blue sky onscreen was replaced by a blanket of rose-colored clouds. Then the camera panned down to show a huge ball of fire that was surfacing above the treetops. There was a sound like the breaking of boards ("I got that by snapping a handful of twigs," Bruce informed them), and Red Rover's head rose from the top of the shed.

Andi's voice took up the narrative: "*Bobby stuck his head out through what was left of the tool-shed roof, and he felt the morning breeze, and he smelled good smells that he hadn't smelled for so long that he had forgotten what they smelled like. He wished that he was a basset so he could bay at the rising sun, but Irish setters can't do that, so he had to make do with singing to the sun in his heart. Then he jumped down to release his friends from captivity.*"

At that point Tim, who had been crouching behind the facade, had given Red a great boost. The dog appeared to literally fly off the roof. Then, with his long ears flapping like wings, he descended slowly ("Mr. Talbert showed me how to make that into slow motion," Bruce said) and landed gracefully in a bed of Mrs. Walker's best yellow tulips. Bruce had replaced the sound of his voice shouting, "Open, sesame!" with a stirring chorus of "We Shall Overcome." Red raced to the door of the shed and lifted the latch, and the dogs poured out in what seemed like an endless stream. Bruce had stepped back with his camera to get a long shot of the exodus, and nobody who was unaware of what was happening behind the facade would have guessed that the same dogs were being sent through that door over and over again.

The music rose to a crescendo, and final credits began to roll.

Red Rover
Snowflake
Lola
Frisky
Bebe
Trixie
MacTavish

Fifi
Foxy
Curly

There had been some discussion about whether to place Curly's name on the list of credits, since he hadn't actually been in the movie, but they had finally agreed that they should include him as a courtesy. Poor Curly could not help that his owner didn't bathe him.

Andi's voice said, *"The dogs lived happily ever after, and Mrs. Rinkle fell into a volcano in China and was never seen again."*

Then the screen went black.

For a moment they all just sat there, too overwhelmed to utter a single word. Then Aunt Alice began to applaud, and the rest joined in, clapping until their palms stung.

Aunt Alice cried, "Author! Author!" and Andi rose proudly to her feet, feeling as if she were accepting an Academy Award.

"I want to thank everyone," she said. "The producers, the actors, and, above all, the wonderful photographer, Bruce Walker!"

"That film ran fourteen and three-quarters

minutes," Tim told them, consulting his watch. "It's just the right length. We got in under the wire."

"In more ways than one," Bruce said. "The deadline's two days from now and we've got to include release forms. Everybody who appears in the film or whose voice is heard has to sign one, so that's Andi and Debbie and Aunt Alice. Do you think we need to get permission from the owners of the dogs?"

"That might be a good idea," Aunt Alice told him. "We can't risk anything that might get this video disqualified."

"I'll get the signatures first thing in the morning," Debbie said. "Now, let's watch the video again. I want to count how many dogs ran out of that shed."

"While you're doing that, I'm going to take an allergy pill," Aunt Alice said. "Just watching those dogs was enough to make me feel like sneezing. Then, in exactly fourteen and three-quarters minutes according to Tim's watch, I'm going to take you all out for ice cream. This calls for a celebration!"

"Hooray!" Andi cried. "I'm starving for a strawberry sundae!"

CHAPTER EIGHT

"Bruce! Wait up!"

Bruce turned automatically at the sound of his name and was surprised to see a slender dark-haired girl elbowing her way through the crowd of students behind him. He and the rest of his classmates were headed to the cafeteria for B lunch. The seventh graders ate first, and the ninth graders last, and eighth grade fell into the middle slot. That meant that the girl had to be in the same grade he was, but he didn't recognize her from any of his classes.

However, because he was naturally polite and because she seemed so determined to talk to him, he stood there like an island in the rushing river of hungry students, waiting for her to catch up with him. When she did, he still didn't recognize her. He took in that she was pretty, and her expressive brown eyes reminded him a bit of Red Rover's.

"Are you sure you've got the right person?" he asked when she caught up to him. "I'm Bruce Walker. I don't think we know each other."

"Of course you don't recognize me," the girl said easily, falling into step beside him as he began to move forward toward the lunchroom, where Tim and his other friends were sure to have staked out a table. "You never looked up from your computer except to look at my computer. I'm Kristy Fernald. We met in the editing bay a couple of weeks ago. My video turned out great. Did yours?"

"Mine looks great, too," Bruce said, relaxing a little now that he knew who she was. "Actually, it's not just my video. It was a group project. My sister wrote the script, and two of our friends helped with the casting and props. My great-aunt was the principal actor. My part was filming and editing. I submitted the video just in time to make the deadline. Having to get releases signed slowed us down a little."

"Weren't those releases the absolute pits?" Kristy said. "I spent two afternoons running all over that retirement home, hunting people down. The bedridden ones were a cinch, but the rest were all over the place — doing water aerobics, playing bridge, or taking watercolor classes. Most of those people are active, and they run around like gerbils."

"I don't understand," Bruce said. "Why did you need to get releases signed? Didn't you make your video to introduce people to the idea of group living?"

"Well, sure," Kristy said. "That was my original reason for making it, but that doesn't mean I can't use it for other things, too. When you told me about that contest, I started talking about it to a really nice boy in my math class, and he got so interested that he looked it up. The next day he gave me all the information about it and suggested that I enter my video. I thought, 'Well, why not?' So I did. There's nothing to lose. I just wanted to thank you for telling me about the contest. I'd never have known about it otherwise."

"But that contest was only for people with dogs!" Bruce exclaimed. "The videos were supposed to be based on the most dramatic event in a dog's life. They weren't about old people taking basket-weaving classes."

"I know exactly what the contest was about," Kristy said, sounding a bit insulted. "I'm not stupid, Bruce! I read the requirements, and my video meets every one of them. It's about my dog's adventures when she visits Glenn Ridge. Lamby — that's short for Lamb Chop — is a therapy dog. I take her to the assisted living home every Saturday. The residents there just love her. They count the days until the weekend, because they know that's when Lamby will be visiting."

"A therapy dog?" Bruce repeated in bewilderment. "Doesn't therapy have to do with helping people exercise? How can a dog do that?"

"That's physical therapy," Kristy said. "That's what my mom does. It's very important for people with physical problems, but emotional therapy's important, too. Lamby cuddles with the patients and gives them kisses and lets them pet her. And she does lots of tricks to entertain them. She's very talented."

To Bruce, she sounded like Andi bragging about Bebe.

"Was that what that scene was about, where all those people were laughing?" Bruce asked. "Your dog was performing tricks?"

"Lamby was dancing at Mrs. Dotson's ninety-ninth birthday party," Kristy said. "The scene after that — I don't think you saw that one — showed her standing on her hind legs, whirling around to the music." She laughed when she saw the confused expression on Bruce's face. "I meant, *Lamby* was whirling, not Mrs. Dotson. Mrs. Dotson uses a walker, but she was singing and clapping her hands and wearing a party hat."

By then they had reached the lunch line, and Bruce was not feeling hungry. The smell of spaghetti surged up from the steaming serving trays, and his stomach started churning. Spaghetti was normally one of his favorite foods, but at that moment he felt the way Andi had felt about her strawberry sundae on the night she'd lost her dream of winning the writing contest.

"Look, Kristy," he said, "no offense, but I'm going to skip lunch today. I don't like the smell of that spaghetti. I'll see you later, okay?"

Kristy's dog-brown eyes looked surprised and hurt. "I was hoping we could eat together and talk about our projects. I've told you all about mine. I want to hear about yours."

"Some other time," Bruce said. "I've got to go talk to a friend of mine. Be careful of that spaghetti."

He stepped out of line and hurried to the far side of the room, to the table where he usually ate. Tim was already there, along with a group of boys they often hung out with. Most of them were almost finished with their lunches.

"Why are you carrying an empty tray?" Tim asked, sliding over on the bench to make room for Bruce to sit down. "I thought spaghetti was your favorite. Is everything all right?"

"Do you see that girl in the jeans and pink shirt?" Bruce asked him. "The one who's getting the fish sticks?"

"The one you walked in with?" Tim said. "Sure, I see her. She's cute. When I saw you talking to her, I thought you might be planning to sit with her."

"That's Kristy Fernald," Bruce said. "She's serious competition. She was in the editing bay at the same time I was, and asked me what I was working on. I was dumb enough to tell her about the contest, and now she's entered it, too!"

"So, what's the big deal?" Tim asked. "We're competing with people from all over the country, even a lot of adults. There's nobody out there with a story that's anything like ours. Nobody has Andi's script or a hero like Red or a villain like your Aunt Alice. We're going to stand out because our production is unique. Besides, we've got an advantage because we're kids. Star Burst Studios will get a lot of publicity if they award first place to exceptional young artists like us and not to grown-ups who have a lot of experience."

"Kristy's an exceptional young artist, too," Bruce said. "She's exactly the same age we are. And what makes her a threat is that her dog's a therapy dog."

"What's that?" Tim asked.

"I never heard of one either," Bruce admitted. "But from what she said, it's sort of like a furry psychiatrist. A therapy dog helps people forget their problems. Kristy takes her dog to the Glenn Ridge Assisted Living Facility every weekend and entertains old people. She's like Mother Teresa, doing good things for humanity. All we did was tell a story about dognapping. She showed real people having fun with her dog at a birthday party. Not just any old birthday, but a ninety-ninth birthday! Her video has a message!"

"So does *Bobby Strikes Back*," Tim reminded him. "It's about an old dog who saves other dogs. It will make people realize that old dogs and old people are important. You can't just shrug them off, because there are things you can learn from them. That makes Andi's story special."

"But Kristy's video is a documentary," Bruce said. "That will shove it up in the ranks ahead of ours. Everything in it is true, not doctored up like ours is."

"That's what she told you," Tim said skeptically. "But what makes you sure it's authentic? Maybe she did some faking just the way we did with Red popping through the roof. She could have gone to that old people's home and filmed some of them having fun at a party and then gone home and inserted some scenes with her dog in them."

"Lamby," Bruce said.

Tim stared at him as if he'd gone crazy.

"What the heck is a *lammy*?"

"That's what she calls her dog," Bruce said. "Her real name is Lamb Chop."

"Nobody weird enough to name her dog Lamb Chop can be trusted," Tim said. "I think Kristy's conning you. I bet she didn't film anything."

"She did," Bruce said. "I saw her working. She's a good editor."

"Okay, so she's a good editor," Tim conceded. "That makes her even more suspicious. Does her original footage have a dog in it or did she edit it in afterward? There's no way for anyone to know that unless they were at the party."

"The people in her scenes were laughing at *something*," Bruce said. "She told me Lamby was dancing."

"*Dancing!*" Tim snorted. "So her dog's not only a shrink but also a dancer? Does Lamby wear a tutu like my sisters do at their ballet recitals? Or maybe she's a tap dancer. That would be impressive — *clickety-click-click* with her toenails on the floor. In our film, you were able to make the sound of the roof breaking by snapping a handful of twigs. Kristy could rap on a board and make it sound like tap dancing."

"I believe her," Bruce said. He didn't know why he felt so certain of Kristy's honesty, but he did. Maybe it was because she had Red Rover's beautiful eyes. Or maybe it was because she had made the effort to find him and thank him. There had been no reason for her to do that. She could have submitted her video without telling him about it.

"Earth to Bruce!" Tim said. "I know she's gotten under your skin, but do you see who she's sitting with?"

"I don't care who she's sitting with," Bruce said. "I hardly even know her. She can sit with anyone she wants."

"Well, you'd better start caring about who her pals are," Tim told him. "She's sitting with Jerry Gordon, and they're laughing together. They look like they're very good friends."

CHAPTER NINE

Neither Bruce nor Andi was in the habit of checking voice mail after school. Since all their friends were in school at the same time they were, there was nobody to call them.

Which was why it was not until their mother arrived home in the late afternoon, having been delayed by a parent-teacher conference at the school where she taught, that anyone bothered to listen to the day's messages. When Mrs. Walker finally did, she was so bewildered by one of them that she listened to it three times before asking Andi, who was seated on the sofa, reading to Bebe, "Do you know where Bruce is?"

"He took Red for a run and brought him back and went out again," Andi said. "Why? Do you need him for something?"

"There's a call for him on our voice mail," Mrs. Walker said. "A Mr. Craig Donovan from Star Burst Studios in California. He wants Bruce to return his call before the end of the day."

"He must be calling about our video!" Andi cried, leaping up from the sofa so abruptly that both Bebe and the book ended up on the floor. "I'll go find Bruce right now!"

She did not have to look far. Her brother was in the driveway, shooting hoops.

"The *Dogs in Action* people phoned while we were at school and left a message!" Andi told him. "That has to mean —" She stopped herself from completing the sentence. She had been preparing to shout, "We made the finals!" but then she remembered having made a similar statement when she'd received the envelope from Pet Lovers Press. She didn't think she could bear to be that disappointed again.

Bruce apparently was remembering that as well, because he was obviously struggling to control his excitement when he asked her, "What did they say?"

"Just for you to call back," Andi said. "Hurry up! I can't stand the suspense! It's like the Pet

Lovers contest all over again, except we know for sure that Jerry didn't enter!"

Their mother was waiting for them in the entrance hall, looking so flustered that Andi suspected that she had continued to listen, over and over again, to the voice message.

"I can't believe this!" Mrs. Walker said. "It never occurred to your dad and me to take this little project seriously. We just thought of it as something you were doing to have fun. Mr. Donovan wants you to call his office immediately!"

"But it's after five!" Bruce said. "Won't his office be closed?"

"There's a three-hour time difference between here and the West Coast," his mother reminded him. "In California it's midafternoon. I wrote the number down for you."

She handed Bruce a slip of paper as reverently as if it were a golden ticket from Willy Wonka's chocolate factory.

Bruce's hand was shaking so hard that he punched the wrong buttons on the phone and had to hang up and start over. When he finally got through, a woman answered, "Star Burst Studios," in a very official voice.

"This is Bruce Walker," Bruce said. "I'm returning a call from Mr. Donovan. . . . Sure, I'll hold. Of course! For however long it takes!" The silence that followed seemed to go on forever. Then Bruce said, "Hello," in a voice that was pitched one octave lower than usual. His voice had just started changing, and he wanted to make sure it didn't squeak.

Andi edged in as close as she could to try to hear the other end of the call. She couldn't make out the words, just a rumbling voice.

"Yes, this is Mr. Walker," Bruce said. "Yes, I own the Irish setter who played Bobby." He paused and then said, "I think so. I mean, I can't imagine why not. Let me check and make sure."

He covered the receiver with his hand and turned to his mother.

"Can I skip school for a couple of days next week? It will just be Thursday and Friday. I'm doing great in all my classes, and it's only a couple of weeks before school's out anyway. Mr. Donovan wants me to bring Red to Hollywood."

"He wants *what*?" Mrs. Walker looked as if she might faint.

"He wants Red and me to go to Hollywood," Bruce repeated. "Our video made the finals, and

Mr. Donovan wants to meet Red and me in person. He says he wants to tape an interview with me and see Red in action."

"And Bebe?" Andi asked eagerly. "Does he want to see Bebe?"

"Afraid not," Bruce said. "He just wants the star dog and its owner. He'll cover all my expenses. Mom, can I go?"

"Give me that phone!" Mrs. Walker snatched the receiver from his hand. "Hello, Mr. Donovan? I'm Linda Walker, Bruce's mother. It's very flattering for you to invite our son to come to Hollywood, but do you realize that Bruce is only fourteen?"

There was a long pause while she listened to Mr. Donovan.

Then she said in a calmer voice, "I understand your confusion. Yes, Bruce is mature for his age and his voice did sound like an adult. I haven't viewed the video yet, but I'm sure it was very well done. Bruce is a fine photographer. Still, as you must understand, we couldn't possibly allow our underage child to go to Hollywood without a chaperone."

Another, much shorter pause.

"That's very kind of you. I'll discuss it with Bruce's father and we'll get back with you. . . . Yes,

I realize the decision must be made immediately. Thank you for honoring Bruce and his accomplishments. He definitely is a special boy. And I think you should know that his younger sister wrote the script."

She said good-bye very calmly and replaced the receiver on the hook. Then she drew a deep, shaky breath and collapsed into a chair.

"What's going on here?" Mr. Walker demanded.

They all had been so glued to the phone conversation that they had not heard the front door open and close. Now Bruce and Andi turned to see their father standing at the entrance to the family room. He set down his briefcase and hurried over to his wife.

"Linda, what's wrong? You look as if you're in shock."

"I suppose I am," Mrs. Walker said in a tremulous voice. "The children's video has made the finals in a national contest. A producer named Craig Donovan wants Bruce to fly to Hollywood. This is surreal! Things like this don't happen to normal people!"

"Surreal is right," Mr. Walker said. "No responsible parents would ship their child off to Hollywood to meet with some stranger. There's no way to know what kind of man this Donovan is or what his true intentions are."

"He sounded sincere," Mrs. Walker said. "He hadn't been aware of Bruce's age. When I told him, he immediately offered to cover the expenses of a chaperone."

"I will be Bruce's chaperone!" Andi volunteered eagerly. "I will protect him from evil and guard him from temptation! I won't let Britney Spears get anywhere near him!"

"Don't be ridiculous," their father said. "He needs an adult chaperone, and neither your mother nor I can get off work. If this opportunity had come after school let out, your mother might have been able to take Bruce to Hollywood. But she can't leave her students in the final days of the school year."

"That's not fair!" Andi cried. "You could make this happen if you wanted to! One of you could quit your job and we could live on welfare until I become a famous writer! This is the best opportunity Bruce will ever have! The two of you are the meanest parents in the world!"

"And you have just placed yourself in the running for being the rudest child in the world," Mr. Walker told her sternly. "We don't allow that sort of talk in our family. Go to your room until you're ready to come down and apologize."

Tears of frustration were streaming down Andi's face as she turned on her heel and stomped angrily out of the room.

"You were very hard on her, John," Mrs. Walker said. "It's understandable that she's upset and disappointed."

"You don't know the half of it," Bruce said. "This was Andi's dream — second only to getting her book published. Of course she's mad! It's not like you didn't know we were making a video and entering it in a contest. Dad, we even invited you to be in it!"

"We're happy to have you and Andi work on creative projects together," Mrs. Walker explained. "It's just that we didn't expect an outcome like this. We assumed that, at most, you'd receive a certificate like Andi did with her book project. That sort of recognition is appropriate for children. But this — it's beyond comprehension! As Dad said, you can't go alone to Hollywood, and neither of us is free to go with you."

"Then the answer is no?" Bruce asked, trying once more. "You won't change your minds? Even if I promise to phone you every half hour to let you know I'm okay?"

"The answer is *no*," his father said. "I'm truly sorry, son. But knowing you made it to the finals should make you proud. That, in itself, is a triumph. After dinner, I think we should go out for ice cream."

"*I apologize*," Andi announced loudly. She had reentered the room while they were talking. "I'd like to go out for ice cream. This time I think I'm going to have a hot-fudge sundae."

"Apology accepted," her father said, putting his arm around her and giving her a hug. "We all sometimes say things we don't mean when we're disappointed. As your mother pointed out, I should have been more sympathetic to what you were feeling."

"Aunt Alice says she'll be happy to chaperone us," Andi said.

Her parents and Bruce stared at her in stunned amazement.

"What?" Mr. Walker exploded. "When did you talk to Aunt Alice?"

"Just now," Andi said. "I used the phone in your bedroom. Aunt Alice said she would love to go to Hollywood, as long as she doesn't have to share a room with a dog. But that's all right, because Mr. Donovan said he would cover the expenses of a chaperone, so Bruce and Red will have one room, and Aunt Alice and I will have the other."

"But Mr. Donovan invited only me!" Bruce protested.

"Aunt Alice said that I should go, too," Andi told him. "She said that's only fair, since I wrote the story. She's going to take me as her guest. Isn't that cool?"

The phone rang.

Mrs. Walker answered it.

"Bruce," she said, "it's for you." She handed him the receiver. "I don't know who this is, but it's definitely not Mr. Donovan."

Bruce said, "Hello?" not bothering to use his deep voice.

"I just got my phone call!" Kristy Fernald said joyfully. "Isn't it great that we're both finalists?"

"Your video's one of the three finalists?" Bruce

shouldn't have been surprised, but in all the excitement he'd forgotten about Kristy. "How did you know that mine was?"

"I asked, of course," Kristy said. "Didn't you ask about me? I'm sure you must have. Mr. Donovan seemed blown away by the fact that we're both from the same small town."

"So you're going to Hollywood next week, too?" Bruce asked her.

"If only!" Kristy said. "But my mom can't get off work to go with me."

"What about your dad?" Bruce asked.

"My parents are divorced," Kristy said. "My dad's out there somewhere, but we haven't heard from him in years. Who's chaperoning you?"

"My dad's Aunt Alice," Bruce said.

He could sense what was coming, and what he suspected was correct.

"I know this is asking a lot," Kristy said, "since your father's aunt doesn't even know me. But do you think she might be willing to chaperone me, too?"

MY ADVENTURES IN HOLLYWOOD — PART ONE

By Andrea Walker

I will get excused absences for the two days of school that I miss if I write a report about my adventures in Hollywood.

So here it is.

It was terrible having to tell my beautiful, talented, brilliant dog, Bebe, that my brother's dog, Red, was going to go to Hollywood with us and Bebe wasn't. It's not Bebe's fault that she isn't able to open gates. If I'd thought about it in time, I could have rewritten the script and made Bobby a dachshund and had him dig a hole and crawl under the gate to get out of his yard. And I could have done something with the toolshed, like make it have a hole in the floor so a dachshund with Bebe's skills and intelligence could have gotten out that way and led the other dogs to safety.

But there was a deadline, and Bruce had all kinds of reasons why Red should be the star, and all of a sudden Red was Bobby, even before I'd written it into the script.

I tried to explain that to Bebe, but she went into one of her sulks and hid behind the clothes dryer in the laundry room, which is what she always does when her feelings are hurt. I didn't even get to kiss her good-bye before we left for the airport.

The plane trip was not as much fun as I'd expected. I wanted to sit with Aunt Alice, but Bruce got there first, so I had to sit with Kristy. Tim told me yesterday that Kristy is Jerry Gordon's girlfriend. That's a scary thing to think about. I kept my arm pulled in tight to my side, because I would smash my way through the plane window and hurl myself out into space before I would brush my elbow against the elbow of a girl whose elbow has touched the elbow of Jerry Gordon.

Kristy brought Lamb Chop on board in a carry-on cage. She put that under the seat in front of her.

Lamb Chop is a Maltipoo. She looks like Snowflake Swanson might look if Snowflake was a midget.

Red had to ride with the luggage.

Right before the plane took off, Kristy's cell phone rang. There was a picture on the screen. Kristy said, "This is so amazing!" Of course that made me curious, so I asked, "What's amazing?" Kristy said, "A boy in my math class told me he's got a cousin in Chicago who looks just like him only older. That cousin just sent me his picture, and it's true! He looks exactly like Jerry, except he has a mustache. Here — look!"

She shoved the phone screen in front of my face before I could stop her, and there was Connor Gordon with fuzz on his upper lip.

"Isn't he cute?" Kristy gushed.

I said, "He has shifty eyes."

"How can you say that?" Kristy asked me, sounding like I'd insulted her dearest friend, even though she's never even met Connor. "This isn't a video, Andi. There's no way you can tell if his eyes are shifting."

Then, thank goodness, there was an announcement for everyone to turn off their cell phones, so Kristy clicked hers off and put it in her purse. I didn't talk to Kristy for the rest of the trip. Instead, I wrote in my notebook. I wrote a poem about how the sky looks from an airplane window and a poem about Bebe in the laundry room. I've decided not to include those poems in this report, because I may want to turn them in as part of a different assignment. For instance, for science we might have to write about cloud formations. There's no sense wasting a poem that I might find a use for later.

When we got to LAX, which is the name of the Los Angeles airport, a man in a uniform was holding up two cardboard signs. One said "WALKER" and the other said "FERNALD." Those were for Bruce and Kristy. Each of them got their own sign, even though we were all going to ride in the same car.

The man got our luggage and let Red out of his crate and took us outside to a limousine. He explained that Mr. Craig Donovan had sent the limo because taxi drivers in Los Angeles won't take dogs as big as Red unless they belong to movie stars. Aunt Alice put on her allergy mask so she could ride in the car with Lamb Chop and Red without sneezing.

We were starving, because the only food on the plane was pretzels in little plastic bags that we couldn't get open. Aunt Alice told us that she used to cut them open with nail scissors, but the man at the airport who put her purse through a metal detector wouldn't let her take her scissors on the plane. Nobody else could do that either, so there were lots of people trying to open the pretzels with their teeth. One woman broke a tooth and started screaming. The flight attendant brought her an ice pack.

It took us over an hour to get to our hotel, because the roads were clogged with traffic. That made it almost bedtime, New Jersey time, and we still hadn't eaten.

We are staying at a special hotel that allows pets and has room service for dogs. Dogs have their own menus. Dry dog food costs eight dollars. Braised beef and garden vegetables costs ten dollars. There is also something called a Grilled Chicken-Liver Feast that's so expensive that Aunt Alice wouldn't let Bruce and Kristy order it for Red and Lamb Chop even though Star Burst Studios is paying for everything. She said it's "inappropriate to take advantage of our hosts."

The limo driver suggested that Aunt Alice take off her mask before she went into the hotel. He was afraid the people at the desk would think it was a holdup. He promised to keep Red and Lamb Chop safe in the car and bring them to Bruce's room after we were registered.

While Aunt Alice was checking us in, a man came up and asked, "Are you here for the Dogs in Action contest?" Aunt Alice said, "Yes," and the man said, "I'm Maynard Merlin, and I'm here for that, too." So we've now met our other competition besides Kristy.

I took notes while our enemy talked to Aunt Alice:

Maynard Merlin has shiny black hair that doesn't match his gray eyebrows.

He was wearing a gray suit and a red tie.

He smiles all the time, even when there's nothing to smile about.

He guessed who we were when he heard Aunt Alice tell the check-in person that we had two dogs outside in a limo.

His own dog, Gabby, was in their room, resting up for tomorrow's interview.

He asked Aunt Alice too many questions.

One question was, could we all eat dinner together? Aunt Alice said that was a nice thought but we were too tired from the long plane trip to be good company and she thought we would order up room service. Then he asked her if she would like to meet him later in the lounge so they could have a drink and get to know each other. She told him, "No, thank you."

Then Kristy asked him what Gabby's video was about.

Mr. Merlin said he'd taught Gabby to talk.

To Be Continued

CHAPTER TEN

They gathered in the hotel lobby at eight o'clock the next morning to wait for the limousine to take them to Star Burst Studios. Maynard Merlin was waiting for the limousine as well, and Gabby was with him. The only one of their group who was not staring at Gabby was Mr. Merlin, who was staring at Aunt Alice.

Aunt Alice adjusted her mask and said, "Good morning, Mr. Merlin."

Mr. Merlin asked, "Is that you, Alice? I didn't recognize you with your facial adornment. I hope you had a good night's rest."

"I slept very well, thank you," Aunt Alice said politely. "Both of our four-legged companions slept in the room with Bruce, so I didn't sneeze even once. Kristy has informed me that Maltipoos are nonallergenic, but I'm not one for taking chances, especially with a big day ahead of us."

The children could not take their eyes off Gabby. They had expected something extraordinary, but he looked like a run-of-the-mill hound-type dog with floppy ears and oversized lips.

Kristy said tentatively, "Hello, Gabby."

Gabby said, "Allo."

Kristy let out a shriek. "Oh, my gosh, he really *does* talk! Mr. Merlin, I thought you were kidding! What else can he say?"

"His vocabulary is somewhat limited, because there are particular sounds that dogs can't make," Mr. Merlin explained. "Gabby has trouble pronouncing certain letters of the alphabet, such as 's' and 'b.' The 'th' sound is beyond him, but he does very well with vowel sounds and with easy letters like 'l,' 'w,' and 'r.'"

"Hello, Gabby," Andi said. "I'm Andi Walker. I'm very glad to meet you."

"Allo, Annie Wawar," Gabby said.

Then, just as Bruce was preparing to introduce himself, the limousine driver arrived to whisk them off to Star Burst Studios.

Aunt Alice took her seat in the car, and Mr. Merlin immediately plunked down next to her. Bruce sat behind them with Red, and Kristy squeezed in beside him with Lamb Chop on her lap. That left Andi to share a seat with Gabby, which she didn't mind at all, as she had liked the dog as soon as she'd seen his sweet face.

"Are you excited about being interviewed?" she whispered to him.

Gabby said, "Uh-uh," and leaned his head against her shoulder.

When they reached the studio, they were ushered into a pleasant waiting room with large plush chairs and a sofa. A secretary phoned Mr. Donovan, who rushed out to greet them. He was wearing a flowered sports shirt and pink pants and had a diamond stud in his right earlobe.

He gave a gasp of startled recognition when he saw Aunt Alice in her face mask.

"Mrs. Rinkle!" he exclaimed. "What a delightful surprise! I was under the impression that you'd fallen into a volcano!"

"I'm not the real Mrs. Rinkle," Aunt Alice told him, extending her hand for him to shake. "I simply played her in the video, which, as you know, is a reenactment, not a documentary. My name is Alice Scudder, and I'm here to act as a chaperone for these three children. These are Bruce Walker, the producer of *Bobby Strikes Back*, and his sister, Andrea, who wrote the film script. This other young lady is Kristy Fernald, who created the video about her therapy dog."

"And I'm Maynard Merlin, and this is Gabby," Mr. Merlin interjected quickly, clearly anxious not to be left out. "Gabby, say hello to Mr. Donovan."

Gabby said, "Allo, Mrrrr Onowam." Apparently *D* and *V* were other letters that caused him problems.

Mr. Donovan appeared both startled and impressed.

"I owe you an apology, Mr. Merlin," he said. "I must admit, I was slightly suspicious that you might have morphed your film in order to create the visual effect of a dog talking. Obviously that's not the case. This is truly astonishing." He turned his attention to the others. "And these glorious animals must be Bobby and Lamb Chop! What marvelous specimens they are!"

"There were other dogs in our video, too," Andi said. "Did you notice the dachshund with the big, expressive eyes? Her name is Bebe, and she can shake hands and roll over."

"I wanna geggit owa wig," Gabby said.

"What he's saying is 'Let's get the show on the road,'" Mr. Merlin translated. "He can't wait to get in front of the camera!"

"No, it's not," Andi said. "He said, 'I want to get this over with.'"

"Well, either way, let's get the ball rolling!" Mr. Donovan said. "The studio in which we'll be taping is down the hall, and I'd like to conduct separate interviews to avoid distractions. Those of you who aren't involved in a taping session are free to relax and make yourselves comfortable out here. Mrs. Rinkle — I mean, Scudder — would you like for my secretary to bring you some coffee?"

"Only if it comes with a straw," Aunt Alice said through the hole in her mask.

"I'm sure that can be arranged," Mr. Donovan said. "In Hollywood all things are possible!" He turned to Mr. Merlin. "I think we should begin with Gabby, since he's so eager to get started. Maynard, I'm going to want you to describe how you trained this extraordinary dog, and, of course, we'll want him to demonstrate his abilities." He turned to Kristy. "I'll be asking you to explain what Lamb Chop does as a therapy dog, and perhaps you can persuade her to dance for us."

"Of course!" Kristy said. "Lamby loves to entertain people. I even brought along her hula skirt."

"As for you, Bruce," Mr. Donovan said, "I'll want you to describe the circumstances behind the story *Bobby Strikes Back*. Bobby's beauty and vitality are truly electrifying. When I saw him come leaping out of the top of that storage shed, I was reminded of famous canine actors such as Rin Tin Tin and Strongheart and Lassie. Bobby has the makings of a star!"

"Thank you, sir," Bruce said.

Once Mr. Donovan took Mr. Merlin and Gabby into the studio and Kristy was occupied dressing Lamb Chop in a grass skirt, Bruce slid over close to Aunt Alice and whispered, "What am I going to tell him? The rules of the contest say the video has to be based on our dog's most dramatic moment, and it is — you can't get much more dramatic than getting dognapped. But Andi did make some changes in details of what happened when she hoped her book would be published as a fictional novel."

"That does create a bit of a problem," Aunt Alice agreed. "However, you can truthfully state that the dognappings occurred last summer and your dog was one of the victims. It might be prudent for Andi to participate in the interview, as she is more at ease with dissembling than you are."

"We can't *lie* to Mr. Donovan!" Bruce protested.

"My gracious, no!" Aunt Alice exclaimed. "I would never suggest that you lie. 'Dissembling' has a different meaning entirely. 'Dissembling' means shrouding negative aspects of a situation and accentuating positive aspects."

"Like with Gabby's talking?" Andi asked, catching on immediately. "He leaves out the parts that don't work, and that makes people pay more attention to the parts that *do* work."

"That's an interesting analogy," Aunt Alice said approvingly. "Andi, you definitely must be part of this interview."

Kristy's cell phone began chiming.

Setting Lamb Chop gently aside, she extracted the phone from her purse.

"It's him again, Andi!" she cried. "This time he's sent me a text message!"

She seemed to believe that Andi would really be interested.

"How special!" Andi said sarcastically, but Kristy accepted the remark at face value and began to read the message aloud. "He says, 'Hi, babe! My cousin, Jerry, says you're hot stuff. Want to get together the next time I'm in Elmwood?'" She paused and then said with bewilderment, "I don't know what Connor means. Why would Jerry tell him I'm 'hot stuff'? I don't even date yet."

"You can't be text messaging Connor Gordon!" Bruce exclaimed. "Are you crazy? That guy's a piece of crud!"

"He looked very nice in the picture he sent," Kristy said. "It isn't kind to judge people by their reputations. Jerry told me that Connor has suffered a lot from people spreading false rumors about him because they're jealous of his sports car."

"That's not the reason!" Bruce turned to Aunt Alice. "*You* tell her about Connor! She'll believe *you*!"

"Kristy, dear," Aunt Alice began, "I would hate

to destroy your commendable faith in humanity, which is one of your most endearing qualities, but it just so happens —"

She was interrupted by the reappearance of Mr. Donovan and Maynard Merlin. Gabby, who looked exhausted, leapt onto a chair and placed his paws over his eyes. He looked as if he were suffering from a terrible headache.

"I hope he didn't overextend himself," Mr. Donovan said. "He was doing great until there at the end when I asked him to recite the Gettysburg Address."

"He'll be fine as soon as he's rested for a while," Mr. Merlin assured him. "The problem with the Gettysburg Address is that it has so many 's' sounds in it. When Gabby hits one of those, he has to find some other sound to substitute, and that creates a drain on his brain. It's like the search-and-replace feature on a computer, except he must do it in his head."

"Well, he did very well," Mr. Donovan said. "I was impressed. Your description of Gabby's training program was mind-blowing. Seven o'clock in the morning until seven at night!"

"If Gabby wants to succeed, he has to practice,"

said Mr. Merlin. "I'm not exactly an ogre. I give him a lunch break."

"Even so, that's a heavy schedule," Mr. Donovan said. "Kristy, I see that you have Lamb Chop garbed in her hula skirt. Are the two of you ready for your interview?"

"Absolutely," Kristy said, stuffing her cell phone back into her purse. "Come on, Lamby! Let's tell the world about therapy dogs!"

Once Kristy and Lamb Chop had left the reception area, Mr. Merlin sat down on the sofa next to Aunt Alice. He reached over and covered her hand with his own.

"How are you holding up, Alice?" he asked gently. "Is this excitement stressing you out?"

"Thank you for your concern, but I'm not stressed out in the least," Aunt Alice told him, sliding her hand out from under his. "I'm in excellent health and enjoying myself tremendously."

"I didn't mean to imply that you weren't looking well," Mr. Merlin said hastily. "It's just that I know it must be stressful to travel with grandchildren."

"Andi and Bruce are my great-niece and great-nephew," Aunt Alice said. "I love them dearly, but they are not my grandchildren. My late husband and I were not fortunate enough to have children."

"So you're all by yourself?" Mr. Merlin exclaimed with sympathy. "It's the same with me. I have no one in my life except Gabby. We share a bachelor apartment, my dog and I, and the evenings are long and lonely."

"Is that why you taught Gabby to talk?" Andi asked him. "So you could have someone to chat with?"

"Yes, but it's not the same as a human companion," Mr. Merlin said. He returned his attention to Aunt Alice. "What is your living situation, Alice? I assume you, too, have an apartment or perhaps a nice condo?"

"I have a three-bedroom home with a rose garden," Aunt Alice told him.

"I'm sure that both are as lovely as their owner," Mr. Merlin exclaimed with enthusiasm. "I have a suggestion to make, and I hope you'll agree to it. Perhaps we could pick up some fast food for the children, and once they are safely stashed in their rooms watching television, you and I could enjoy a candlelight dinner in the rooftop-garden restaurant at our hotel."

"Mr. Merlin, I am flattered by your attention, but I must advise you that I have been spoken for," Aunt Alice said.

Mr. Merlin seemed stunned. "You're telling me you're engaged?"

"A delightful gentleman asked me to marry him," said Aunt Alice. "I don't mean to imply that you are not also a delightful gentleman, but this other gentleman found me first, and finders — as they say — are keepers."

"Then that mask has some sort of religious significance?" Mr. Merlin asked, apparently reeling with shock from this sudden disclosure. "I've heard about cultures in which women, once they are betrothed, must keep their faces covered until after the marriage ceremony."

"Cultural customs are fascinating," Aunt Alice agreed. She inserted the straw through the mask so she could suck her coffee, which put an end to further conversation.

Mr. Donovan returned to the room with Kristy and Lamb Chop.

"Bruce, it's your turn!" he said. "It's time for you and this beautiful setter to tell and show the world how Bobby struck back."

"I was hoping that maybe my sister could come with me," Bruce said. "She might think of things to tell you that I've forgotten."

"There's no need for that," Mr. Donovan assured him. "You and Bobby will do just fine on your own."

"Mr. Donovan, I'd like to suggest —" Aunt Alice broke in, but Kristy interrupted her.

"That's not fair, Mr. Donovan!" she burst out. "Andi wrote the script! There wouldn't be any *Bobby Strikes Back* without Andi! It's only right for you to interview Bruce and Andi both!"

Andi turned to stare at her enemy in amazement.

Maybe she's not so bad after all, she thought reluctantly.

MY ADVENTURES IN HOLLYWOOD — PART TWO

By Andrea Walker

Mr. Donovan's studio was not what I'd always pictured when people said the word "Hollywood." It was just a room with a chair and a couch and three cameras, one aimed at the chair and two at the couch. One man ran all the cameras.

Mr. Donovan told Bruce and me to sit on the couch with Red between us. The cameraman attached little microphones to the front of our shirts. Then Mr. Donovan asked the cameraman, "Where's the gate?" The cameraman said, "I think they're still putting the latch on it."

He left the room and came back with a piece

of plywood that had a fake gate in it. It was a facade.

Mr. Donovan sat down in the chair and told the cameraman, "Roll 'em." Then he smiled at one of the cameras and said, "In the studio with us today are Bruce Walker, producer of Bobby Strikes Back; his sister, Andrea; and the heroic Bobby. Bruce, please share with our viewers the story of your brave dog" — he gestured at Red, who was staring straight into the camera lens just like Mr. Donovan — "this courageous animal who was dognapped by a deranged woman and held captive in a toolshed."

"Well," Bruce began. I knew from the tone of his voice that he was going to say all the wrong things. "Bobby's real name is Red Rover. The dognappers were two teenage boys, and they weren't deranged, just evil. And the toolshed was really a chicken coop. But the rest of what you just said was right."

"Do you mean Mrs. Rinkle was not the dog-napper?" Mr. Donovan asked him.

At that point Bruce went blank. He had not been listening to Aunt Alice when she had dissembled to Mr. Merlin, so he'd missed out on a valuable demonstration.

I knew it was my job to save him.

"When I wrote the script, I had to make a few changes," I said. "The real dognappers were juveniles, and I thought it might not be legal to expose them to the public. I didn't want Star Burst Studios to be sued, so I combined them and made them Mrs. Rinkle."

"But the dogs in your video were playing their own parts, were they not?" Mr. Donovan asked.

"Oh, yes," I assured him. "Except for that beautiful dachshund, Bebe. She was an understudy, substituting for Bully Bernstein, who was having a birthday party. Bully's the one who got dognapped, but it could just as well have been Bebe, because the Gordon boys were snatching every dog they could get their hands on."

"We would have liked to use a chicken coop," Bruce said. "But we didn't have the wire mesh, so we couldn't build one. The toolshed was just a facade, like that one over there that your cameraman just brought in."

Mr. Donovan didn't look as happy as he had in the beginning.

"But in the real event," he said, "Bobby — or Red Rover or whatever this dog's name is — did release his captive companions, is that correct?"

"Red saved himself and all the rest of the dogs," I told him. That was not a lie at all, because the sound of Red barking was what had led us to the chicken coop.

"And he does know how to open a latch?" Mr. Donovan asked me.

"Oh, yes!" I assured him.

Mr. Donovan turned to Bruce.

"Is it all right with you if we put Red Rover to the test?"

"Sure," Bruce said. "Red will do almost anything I tell him to."

The cameraman hauled the facade to the front of the room so all the cameras could focus on it. Then Bruce told Red, "Open, sesame!" and Red raced over and opened the gate.

Mr. Donovan had Bruce tell Red to do that three times so the cameraman could take pictures from lots of different angles. One of them was just a close-up picture of Red's teeth when he pulled up the latch.

Then we went back to the waiting room, where the secretary had brought in lunch. Aunt Alice couldn't eat it because of her mask, and Gabby was too tired, but the rest of us gobbled it up. The desserts were cupcakes with dog faces.

Just before we left to go back to our hotel, Mr. Donovan told us, "Our intention is to air all three videos on national television, along with the interviews I conducted with you today. Then we'll have our viewers call a free eight-hundred number to vote for their favorite star dog. I think we have everything we need except for one release form."

"Oh, no!" Kristy said. "Don't tell me I missed somebody!"

"Not you," Mr. Donovan said. "The form we're missing is for Bobby Strikes Back. We need a release from the blond young man on the skateboard who appears in the background of all the scenes with Mrs. Rinkle in them. Bruce, please get that taken care of as soon as you get home. We can't air a video unless we have releases from everyone."

The next morning, Mr. Merlin and Gabby were in the hotel lobby, checking out at the same time we were.

Mr. Merlin gave Aunt Alice his business card. He told her he lives in Philadelphia, which isn't terribly far from Elmwood, and if her "life plan changes," he would like very much to get to know her better.

Aunt Alice told him her life plan is set in concrete.

While they were talking, I went over to say goodbye to Gabby. I whispered an important message in his ear.

He looked at me with the saddest eyes in the world and licked my hand.

The End

CHAPTER ELEVEN

When Jerry answered the door, Bruce got straight to the point.

He said, "I'm here to ask you to sign a release form."

"A release form?" Jerry asked in surprise. Then a light of understanding broke over his face. "Oh, I get it! It's those ownership papers my dad signed over to you. Did those require my signature? If so, then Red's still legally mine!"

"No way!" Bruce said. "Those papers were in your dad's name, because he's the one who bought Red in the first place. Red's mine, free and clear. This is about the video I taped in our backyard. You're in the background, cruising back and forth on your skateboard. I was so intent on the filming that I didn't notice what was going on in the alley. Now I've got to get signed releases from everybody who appears in the film, whether they were supposed to be there or not. And that includes you."

"You mean you've sold that video!" Jerry exclaimed. "How much are you getting for it? If I sign a release, I'm going to want my share."

"We're not getting paid," Bruce said. "Since Andi didn't win the contest with her book, I made this video as a way to help her get her story told. Give my sister a break! It's no skin off your nose if *Bobby Strikes Back* is on television. This won't interfere with the fame and money you'll be getting from your book."

"There's got to be a prize for winning that contest," Jerry said. "If it isn't money, what is it?"

"The dog who stars in the winning video will be given a chance to audition for films," Bruce said. "But we haven't won the contest. All we've done is make it into the finals. Viewers will vote on the winner."

"I might consider signing that release," Jerry said.

"You will?" Bruce couldn't believe what he was hearing. Was it possible that Jerry's success had made him less greedy?

"I said I *might*," Jerry said. "But I'm not going to do it for nothing. If you can't afford to pay me, then maybe we can trade off services. You do a favor for me, and I do one for you."

"What do you mean?" Bruce asked suspiciously.

"When I won the young author contest, I thought Pet Lovers Press would buy my story and publish it and that would be that," Jerry said. "I never guessed they'd expect me to do more work on it. They sent my manuscript back, and the editor's got it plastered with Post-it notes. She wants me to make all kinds of ridiculous changes. She says the wording is too old-fashioned, and there's a train wreck where a dog gets killed, and that's too traumatic for little kids. I didn't even remember that scene was in the book."

"So what are you saying?" Bruce asked. "What kind of trade-off do you want?"

"Your sister likes to do writing projects," Jerry said. "How about she takes this manuscript and makes it like the editor wants it, and then I sign the release form?"

"Don't you want to do your own revisions?" Bruce asked him. He knew how possessive Andi was about *Bobby Strikes Back*. There was no way she ever would have allowed someone else to make changes.

"I don't have time for that sort of busywork," Jerry said. "My publicist is lining up radio and TV interviews. He's trying to get me on *Oprah* and *Good Morning America*, and even the *Eileen Stanton Show*. I'm going to be busy all summer promoting my book. It's an even trade — Andi helps me, and I help her."

Bruce struggled to contain his fury. How could Jerry consider the few seconds it would take him to sign a release form comparable to the hours — or maybe even days or weeks — that it would take Andi to revise his manuscript? And to add insult to injury, it was the same manuscript that had kept her own book from being published!

But this wasn't his call to make.

"Get me the manuscript," he said. "I'll take it to Andi, and she can read it and make her own decision."

"That's cool," Jerry said with a grin. "I'm sure she'll say yes. What choice does she have? Wait here a minute and I'll get it for you."

He disappeared into the house and came out with a thick pile of pages so sprinkled with yellow Post-it notes that the manuscript looked like it had been attacked by a flock of butterflies.

"Let me know by tomorrow," Jerry said. "If Andi won't do it, I'll give the job to Sarah. She's a very fast typist, probably faster than Andi."

"Who's Sarah?" Bruce asked, mentally running through the roster of girls in their English class and finding no Sarah among them.

"She's one of Connor's girlfriends in Chicago," Jerry said. "She's got a huge crush on him and will do anything for him. I'm sure she'd be thrilled to work on his cousin's manuscript. So if Andi wants this release signed, she'd better jump at this opportunity. Otherwise it goes to Sarah."

"I can do this," Andi said as she riffled through the manuscript, reading the notes on the Post-its.

"It looks like a ton of work," Bruce said doubtfully.

"Yes, it does, but the editor's suggestions make sense," Andi said. "Like this one: 'Does this dog have to die in the train wreck, or might he be knocked unconscious and rejoin his companions in a later chapter?' I don't want that dog to die either. I'd love to make him come alive again and put him back in the story."

"Then you want me to tell Jerry yes?" Bruce asked her.

"Of course," Andi said. "School lets out next week, and I can work on this all day every day. It will give me a chance to learn how to work with an editor."

"I hate to think of you doing Jerry's grunt work," Bruce said.

"It's better than tennis camp," Andi said. "Last night, when I came downstairs to get Bebe a snack, I heard Mom and Dad talking in the living room. They think that going to tennis camp will make me 'more sociable and well-adjusted.' I was trying to think of a way to get out of it. Now I can tell them I can't go because I've got a job."

It took Andi two weeks to make the changes the editor had asked for, and those weeks were filled with surprises. For one thing, Jerry turned out to be a gifted writer. For another, she was amazed at his apparent affection for dogs and his ability to empathize with their emotions. He had written *Ruffy*

Dean Joins the Circus from Ruffy's viewpoint, and the story really did sound as if it had been written by a dog. *"One hot June day, while merrily sleuthing a dried-up chicken head in Mrs. Dean's pet pansy bed (oh, how she loved to have me dig in that pansy bed!), I swallowed a bumblebee,"* Ruffy said. The editor suggested that it would make more sense if Ruffy swallowed a honeybee, which Andi thought was a reasonable suggestion, since it happened in a flower bed. But she couldn't get over that even if Jerry had chosen the wrong bee, he had written that scene so well. Ruffy's description of *"trying frantically to tie myself into seventeen kinds of knots and simultaneously imitate a high-powered pin-wheel in full motion"* when the bee stung the lining of his stomach made her cringe with sympathy.

Even though the style *did* seem a bit old-fashioned, *Ruffy Dean Joins the Circus* was definitely a good story.

In a way, this made Andi feel better about losing the contest, because *Bobby Strikes Back* had been up against strong competition. In another way, it made her feel worse, because now she had no true reason to feel angry about losing to the person she hated most in the world. She had once promised herself that if she ever met a boy who felt the same way that she did about writing, she would marry him when she grew up. It was sickening to think that her future husband might have to be Jerry.

Mr. Donovan called twice, wanting to know why he hadn't received the release form. The first time, Bruce took the call and assured him, "I'll have it for you soon." The second time, Andi took the phone call. She tried to think of a way to dissemble, but the challenge was too great, and she ended up telling a straight-out lie.

"We mailed it last Friday," she said. "Haven't you gotten it yet? Maybe it's been lost in the mail. We'll get that boy to sign another release form, but we'll have to wait until his hand heals. He broke all his fingers in a garbage disposal."

"How long do you think it will be before he can sign his name?" Mr. Donovan asked her.

"About three days," Andi told him, assessing the stack of pages she still had to work on. "His cast will be off on Tuesday, and we'll get that release form into the mail to you on Wednesday."

Three days later, she and Bruce walked down the block to Jerry's house and delivered the manuscript.

Jerry accepted it, said, "Thanks," and started to shut the door.

"Hang on there a minute!" Bruce said, sticking his foot in the crack to prevent the door from closing all the way. "It's payback time. I've got a release for you to sign."

"That will have to wait," Jerry said. "I'm too busy right now."

"Are you joking?" Bruce demanded. But he knew that Jerry wasn't joking. Jerry never joked.

"No," Jerry said, "I'm just overwhelmed by commitments. Next week I'm going to be on the *Eileen Stanton Show*. Pet Lovers Press is going to fly me to New York and put me up in a five-star hotel. Connor's going to drive there to meet up with me. We've both got fake IDs, and we're going to do the town, and I don't mean the Statue of Liberty and the Empire State Building."

"It will take you five seconds to sign this release," Bruce said. "We made a deal. Andi's done her part. Now it's your turn."

"Andi did *not* do her part," Jerry said. "This manuscript's not retyped. All your sister did was scribble stuff in the margins. Even a monkey could do that. Or a dog with a pencil in its mouth. If I'd had any sense, I'd have had Connor give this to Sarah."

"The manuscript wasn't supposed to be retyped!" Andi told him. "Didn't you read the editor's letter? She said to make corrections in the margins."

"What's wrong with you, Jerry?" Bruce demanded, his voice shaking with anger. "Andi did her job perfectly. Now you do yours!"

"Stop trying to make me out to be a bad guy," Jerry said, all of a sudden giving them one of his sweet smiles. "I'm willing to sign that release so your video can be aired. But there's one more thing I'll need from you before I do that."

"What?" Bruce asked apprehensively.

"Red Rover," Jerry said.

CHAPTER TWELVE

"Don't get me wrong — I'm not asking you to give me my dog back for nothing," Jerry said. "You paid my dad for him, and I'll reimburse you. I got a check from Pet Lovers Press, so I can afford to do that. If Red has a chance of becoming a movie star, I want him back."

Bruce was too shocked to respond. He opened and closed his mouth, but his voice wouldn't work.

Andi was not affected by any such problem.

"Absolutely *not!*" she said firmly. "We will *never* give up Red Rover!"

"I thought getting your video on this show meant a lot to you," Jerry said. His smile was now more of a smirk. "Don't you want your little story to be on TV?"

"Not in exchange for a member of our family!"

Andi said. "Red belongs to Bruce. We will never sell him, especially to somebody who tortures animals."

Bruce knew that he ought to say something, but he was so choked up with fury that he couldn't get the words out. Besides, Andi was doing just fine. She was on a roll.

"And I'm never going to marry you," Andi added as an afterthought. "I wouldn't do that if you were the only boy writer in the world!"

Now Jerry and Bruce were both too stunned to respond.

"Give me back that manuscript and I'll erase all my notes," Andi continued. "You can do your own work or give it to Connor's friend Sarah."

"No way," Jerry said. "I'm keeping it just the way it is. The editor's going to be impressed by how fast I got the work done. As for marrying you — are you crazy? Where did that idea come from? Nobody will ever marry a fat nerd like you."

Bruce's voice clicked on and was working again.

"My sister is *not* a fat nerd!" he shouted in fury.

He turned to look at Andi and realized it was true. She used to be overly plump, but that wasn't the case now. He had gotten so used to thinking of her as pudgy that he hadn't noticed how much she had changed in the past year. She wasn't as slender as Kristy, but she looked okay. In fact, she looked good.

It gave him a jolt to realize his sister was growing up.

"Get your foot out of the door or I'll slam it on you," Jerry said.

This was a major threat, because Jerry had muscles. Since Bruce was showing no signs of moving his foot, Andi bent down and yanked it to safety.

She did that just before the door to the Gordons' house crashed shut.

Bruce was still holding the unsigned release form in his hand.

"I'm sorry, sis, but I guess that's it," he said helplessly. "We've used every weapon in our arsenal."

"Not quite," Andi said. "We've still got Kristy."

"How does Kristy fit into this?" Bruce asked her.

"She and Jerry are friends," Andi said. "Maybe she could talk him into changing his mind."

Bruce's first impulse was to say, "I don't want Kristy involved in this." Then he thought about how loyal Andi had been to him a few minutes ago.

She hadn't thought twice about giving up her dream to protect Red.

"Okay, I'll ask Kristy," he said. "But I don't think she'll do it. She's not going to want to get caught between us and Jerry."

However, when he phoned Kristy, her reaction surprised him.

"This has to be a misunderstanding," she said. "Jerry would never do anything that mean to anybody. I'll go over to his house right now and talk to him. Leave it to me. I'll get this mistake straightened out."

A half hour later, the doorbell rang. Bruce opened the door to find Kristy standing on the porch.

"He won't do it," she said. "He's furious at Andi. He says she doesn't deserve to have her story on television."

"Did he tell you why he feels that way?" Bruce asked her.

"He said Andi's so jealous of his winning that writing contest that she tried to destroy his manuscript," Kristy said. "She begged him to let her read it, because she wanted to see what a prizewinning story was like so she could become a better writer. He let her borrow it, because he wanted to help her. He said she took the manuscript home and kept it for ages, and when she finally returned it, she'd scribbled all over it. It's now such a mess he's afraid the publisher won't want it. He showed me the manuscript, and it does have writing in the margins."

"Jerry asked Andi to make those corrections," Bruce said. "He's mad at her and me both, but not about that. It's because he wants Red Rover, and we won't let him have him. He wants to own a dog that's a Hollywood star."

Kristy was silent for a moment as she took that in.

Then she exclaimed, "What a jerk!"

"You mean you believe me instead of Jerry?" Bruce asked incredulously. "Isn't Jerry your boyfriend?"

"Are you kidding?" Kristy exclaimed. "He's just a boy from my math class. I thought he was nice, but I sure don't think so now. I'll always believe you and Andi. Anybody related to your Aunt Alice must be trustworthy."

"Well —" Bruce didn't quite know how to respond to that statement. "Maybe you shouldn't always totally believe Andi, but this time she's telling the whole truth. She didn't ask for that manuscript; Jerry gave it to her. He said if she made those corrections, he'd sign the release form. Now he says he won't sign it unless I sell him Red."

"Can we edit Jerry out of the video?" Kristy suggested.

"I thought about that, but there's no way to do it," Bruce told her. "He's in the background of all the scenes with Mrs. Rinkle in them, and if we cut those, there won't be any story left. Besides, now that school's out, we can't use the editing bay. And we won't have Mr. Talbert to help us."

"Is there anyone else who might talk to Jerry?" Kristy asked. "What about his cousin, Connor? He looked so sweet in the picture he sent to my cell phone."

"Connor!" Bruce exclaimed in horror. "He's even worse than Jerry!"

"Do you think it would help if I called him anyway?" Kristy asked. "I have his number from his text message. Jerry told him that I'm 'hot stuff.' I could offer to send him my picture if Jerry signs that release."

"Connor's got pretty girls hanging all over him," Bruce said. "He's not going to do you a favor just to get your picture. The only person who might have influence is Aunt Alice. Last summer Connor pushed her down and dislocated her shoulder. She didn't press charges, but she did file a report with the police."

"Let's go ask her to phone Connor and threaten to charge him with assault and battery!" Kristy cried.

Before Bruce realized what was happening, she had grabbed his hand and was dragging him down the porch steps and onto the sidewalk. He had never held hands with a girl before and had always wondered if his hand would sweat if he did. Kristy's hand was so cool that it wasn't a problem. All in all, he found the experience rather pleasant.

Aunt Alice was in her yard, kneeling in the dirt, planting flowers. She looked pleased to see them, but also a little surprised.

Bruce hastily dropped Kristy's hand and stuffed his own hand into his pocket.

"Hello, Mrs. Scudder!" Kristy said. "Would you please phone Connor Gordon and make him force Jerry to sign the release so *Bobby Strikes Back* can be on television? Maybe you could threaten to have him put in jail for shoving you."

"Nothing would give me more pleasure than to blackmail Connor," Aunt Alice said, laying down her trowel. "However, it would serve no purpose. As we learned from Jerry when we were filming the dog-stuffing scene, those boys are too egotistical to take threats seriously. Bruce, you might ask your father to talk to Mr. Gordon, but I doubt that that will work either. Jerry has his parents wrapped around his little finger."

"So our video can never be aired," Bruce said despondently.

"It sounds that way," said Aunt Alice. "I'm just as upset as you are. All those 'ha, ha, has' just going to waste."

"I feel awful for Andi," Kristy said. "She must feel terrible. Now it will be just my video and Mr. Merlin's."

"I don't think Andi will crash the way she did when she didn't win the writing contest," Aunt Alice said. "She's learning how to deal with disappointment. I've also been having some thoughts about Mr. Merlin. I believe the time has come to run a background check on him."

"How do you know how to do that?" Kristy asked her.

"Aunt Alice is a private investigator," Bruce said proudly.

He helped his great-aunt to her feet, and she pulled off her garden gloves and led the way into her house and up the stairs to her office.

"*Maynard Merlin,*" she said as she switched on her computer. "I've been meaning to check him out ever since we got back from Hollywood. I just haven't gotten around to it. Maynard Merlin — Maynard Merlin — "

She kept clicking from Web site to Web site.

"Why do you want to run a background check?" Bruce asked her.

"I became curious when he gave me his card," Aunt Alice said. "It had his name and address, but not the name of his business. I started to wonder if he might be a professional ventriloquist and that's how he makes Gabby talk."

She clicked around some more.

Then she said, "My suspicions were wrong. Mr. Merlin appears to be unemployed. I see nothing to indicate that he has a background in ventriloquism."

"So Gabby's for real!" Kristy said. "I'm glad to know that. I just love Gabby. When I told him good-bye, he licked my hand."

"He didn't say 'Goowye'?" Bruce asked in surprise.

"No, he just licked me like a regular dog," Kristy said. "Andi said good-bye to him first and whispered in his ear, so maybe he was thinking about whatever it was she said to him."

Aunt Alice had continued to pull up Web sites.

"This is interesting," she said, frowning a little. "It explains how Mr. Merlin can get along so well without holding a job. He's been married five times, each time to an elderly widow with a house and other assets. Mr. Merlin has apparently inherited from all of them."

CHAPTER THIRTEEN

LOCAL PRODIGY TO APPEAR ON NATIONAL TELEVISION

Jerry Gordon, 14, hopes his appearance on national television will encourage other young writers to follow their dreams.

Jerry, whose novel, *Ruffy Dean Joins the Circus*, was awarded first place in the Young Author Dog Lovers Contest, sponsored by Pet Lovers Press, will appear tonight on the *Eileen Stanton Show* to share this experience with the world.

The popular television show, which is filmed in New York, will air at 8 P.M. EST.

"I want to inspire other kids who want to be writers!" Jerry said in a recent interview with the *Elmwood Tribune*. "It takes hard work and dedication, but it's worth it."

Jerry's parents, Gerald and Emily Gordon, are proud of their son's accomplishment but did not accompany him to New York.

"This is Jerry's big moment, not ours," Gerald Gordon said. "He told us he wanted to make this trip on his own, and we agreed that he's earned the right to do that. We trust our son implicitly. Any young man who can get a book published at the age of 14 doesn't need a babysitter."

There was a lot of talk at the Walkers' dinner table that night about whether to watch the show. Mr. Walker voted no. He was irate about the way Mr. Gordon had reacted to his polite request for help in persuading Jerry to sign the release form.

"He refused to take the situation seriously," he told the family. "His view is that parents shouldn't get involved in spats between children, and young people ought to work out their problems on their own. When I told him that Bruce and Andi had tried to do that, he said, 'Well, maybe they didn't try hard enough.'"

Mrs. Walker was upset about that as well, but she also wanted to watch the program.

"What good would it do us to boycott it?" she asked reasonably. "That's not going to stop it from being shown. Everybody else in town is going to be watching it, so why shouldn't we?"

Eileen Stanton was her favorite talk show host. Mrs. Walker never missed her show if she could help it.

Bruce was feeling so miserable about his phone conversation that afternoon with Craig Donovan that the very thought of Jerry made his stomach lurch. Mr. Donovan had been stunned to learn that Bruce was unable to provide the signed release form.

"Your sister assured me the cast would be off by now!" he said.

"The cast?" Bruce repeated blankly.

"The cast on the boy's hand. Were there further complications? I don't suppose you have an orthopedic hand specialist in Elmwood?"

"I don't know," Bruce said. "In fact, I don't even know what one is."

"Where is that poor boy now?" Mr. Donovan asked him. "Perhaps we could get him to make an *X* with his left hand and have a notary public witness it. That would be the legal equivalent of a signature."

"If you mean the boy on the skateboard, he's in New York," Bruce said.

"They have good doctors in New York," Mr. Donovan said approvingly. "But that won't help us in this dire situation. We'll be airing the videos on Dog Appreciation Day, which is only a week away. It's an hour-and-a-half show, which allows us time for three fifteen-minute videos, three interviews, and the necessary commercials. Now, with only two videos in the competition, what are we going to do with the rest of the time?"

"Maybe you could sell more commercials?" Bruce suggested.

"It's too late for that," Mr. Donovan said. "What we need is additional talent to fill the void. I read in the paper about a teenage boy who's written a book about a circus dog. I'll try to track him down. Maybe he'll agree to appear on the show in between the two videos."

"I can't tell you how bad I feel about this," Bruce said.

He had never been so humiliated in his life.

Mr. Donovan was a nice man, and Star Burst Studios had invested a lot of money in bringing Bruce, Aunt Alice, and Red Rover to Hollywood.

He felt terrible about letting them down, but he felt even worse for Andi, who had twice come so close to her dream and now had been thwarted a second time.

Still, he voted yes to watching the *Eileen Stanton Show*. As his mother had said, there was nothing to be gained by not watching it, and he couldn't help being curious about what Jerry would say.

Andi didn't participate in the conversation. She knew that the family would end up watching the show.

Which of course they did, although they all cringed a little when Jerry appeared on the screen. He looked even more adorable than he did in real life. His cheeks were flushed from the color applied by the makeup artist, his lashes had been darkened by mascara, and his hair had been sprayed with something that made it glisten.

His flashing smile lit up the studio, and Eileen Stanton, who could usually upstage anybody, seemed a little bit drab in contrast, despite her orange blouse and flaming red hair.

She was obviously smitten with Jerry, especially when he raised her hand to his lips and kissed it.

"What inspired you to write your story from the

viewpoint of a dog?" she asked, leaning eagerly forward for his answer.

"I've always had a special kinship with dogs," Jerry said. "It's as if I can see into their souls. Ruffy's story poured forth from my fingertips in a magical way. The words popped onto the screen as if Ruffy himself was dictating them. I've been told that that's the way Shakespeare wrote his plays — not on a computer, of course, but with a quill pen. And Hemingway did that too, and Gene Simmons and R. L. Stine and the Gospel writers in the Bible. It's the sign of — of —"

He paused, as if embarrassed to go on.

Eileen Stanton completed the sentence for him.

"Of *genius*!" she said reverently.

"Oh, I wouldn't say that exactly," Jerry told her modestly. "I'm just a normal kid with big dreams and aspirations. I want to introduce other kids to the joy of writing and the appreciation of good literature."

"Tell us about Ruffy's circus," Eileen Stanton begged him. "Please describe it in your own vivid words so our viewers and I can visualize it just the way you do."

"It was just a regular circus," Jerry told her, seeming slightly uncomfortable for the first time since he had stepped onto the set. "You know what they're like — with elephants and clowns and pretty girls on trapezes. I hope you don't mind if I don't go into more detail. I don't want to spoil the story for people who buy the book."

"I read in the press release that the second-place winner, Amanda Wallace, is even younger than you are," Eileen Stanton said. "We had hoped to have her join you on the show but weren't able to locate her. Have you been in touch with her? I should think the two of you would have a lot in common."

"No, we haven't talked," Jerry said. "When I read her name in the paper, I wanted to call and congratulate her, but I couldn't find her phone number."

"We need to take a commercial break, and then we'll take calls from our viewers," Eileen Stanton said, regretfully tearing her eyes away from Jerry to gaze into the camera lens. "I'm sure there are lots of people who would love to speak to our guest. What an inspiration he is to the young people of our nation!"

Mr. Walker pushed the MUTE button.

"I knew I should have phoned the paper and corrected that error!" he said. "*Amanda Wallace?* Of course they weren't able to find Andi!"

"I wouldn't have wanted to be on that show

anyway," Andi said. "How could I sit there while Jerry compared himself to Shakespeare? And it's weird the things he was saying about Ruffy's circus. It didn't have clowns and elephants and acrobats."

"No elephants?" her mother exclaimed. "You must be mistaken, honey. Every circus has elephants."

"Not Ruffy's circus," Andi said. "There was nobody in it but dogs. Ruffy did tricks like Lamb Chop does at the retirement home. In the story, the dogs' master takes them from town to town in a car. How could you squeeze an elephant into a car?"

The commercials were over. Mr. Walker activated the sound again, and calls began to flood in.

The first was from a teacher who wanted to know if Jerry did school visits. Jerry said he might consider that if he was paid enough.

Then a man who raised elephants as a hobby called to inform people that an elephant's hair was too tough to be cut by razors and had to be shaved with a blowtorch. He wanted to know if Jerry had included a blowtorch scene in his book.

Jerry said no, but he'd be sure to include one in the sequel.

Then, suddenly, there was a voice that all of them recognized.

"I'm Alice Scudder," the voice said. "I am calling to correct an error. The girl who came in second in the Young Author Dog Lovers Contest, with a brilliant story titled *Bobby Strikes Back*, is *not* named Amanda Wallace. She is Andrea Walker, the daughter of John and Linda Walker of Elmwood, New Jersey. Andi has been writing since she was much younger than Jerry Gordon. She published her first poem when she was ten."

"I appreciate your setting us straight, Ms. Scudder," Eileen Stanton said. "That mix-up in names must be the reason no one could find her."

"It may be the reason that *you* couldn't find her," Aunt Alice said. "However, Jerry knows Andi personally. He asked her to do revisions on *Ruffy Dean Joins the Circus*. Jerry made a deal with Andi that if she would do his work for him —"

"Thank you, Ms. Scudder," Eileen Stanton interrupted hastily. "We appreciate your call, but we need to move on. Our phones are ringing off the hooks!"

The next call was from a girl who wanted to know if Jerry had a girlfriend.

Jerry blushed endearingly.

"I've been so busy with my writing that I haven't

had a chance for that," he told her. "Maybe now I ought to make up for lost time."

The audience laughed and applauded, and the girl squealed and tried to give him her phone number. Eileen Stanton told her to leave it with the operator, who would see that Jerry got it after the show. Then five more girls called in to announce that they, too, were leaving their numbers with the operator and wanted Jerry to call them.

One, a drama major at a conservatory for dramatic arts, suggested that she and Jerry get together to read Shakespeare. Jerry said that would be fun, but he was overcommitted.

Music began to play as the show reached its close.

"Thank you, Jerry Gordon, for being with us tonight," Eileen Stanton said. "I know your book is going to be a bestseller. I plan to buy copies for everybody I know!"

And then she got up and hugged him, right there in front of the camera.

"Yuck!" Andi said, and covered her eyes with her hands.

"Double yuck," Mrs. Walker said, putting her arm around her daughter and hugging her tight. "I will never watch that ridiculous show again."

CHaPteR FouRteen

The week that led up to Dog Appreciation Day dragged by so slowly that it was as if time had become stuck.

As heartsick as they were that *Bobby Strikes Back* would not be shown, Bruce and Andi were anxious to see the other two videos. Tim and Debbie were equally curious, especially after hearing about Gabby's unique talent.

"I won't believe a dog can talk until I hear it with my own ears," Tim said.

The four of them gathered at Aunt Alice's house to watch the program. They had invited Kristy to join them, but she said it was going to be shown on the big-screen TV in the recreation room at Glenn Ridge, and she thought that she and Lamb Chop should view it with the residents.

"Mrs. Dotson is terribly excited," Kristy told

them. "Not everybody's ninety-ninth birthday party is on national television!"

When they consulted the paper, they learned that the show had been reduced to one hour. Apparently Mr. Donovan had not been able to reach Jerry in time to include him on the program.

Kristy's video was the first to be shown, and it was very well done. It started with an overview of the Glenn Ridge facility — a comfortable living room, a dining room, a recreation room, a therapy room, a swimming pool, and a library.

Kristy's voice narrated the virtual tour, describing Glenn Ridge as a *"home for people who can no longer do all the things they did when they were young."* She continued: *"They need help with some day-to-day activities, but they still want to live full lives. They swim and play games and take classes, and there's a van that takes them to concerts and movies and the mall. And sometimes they have special guests."*

When Kristy said the word "guest," Lamb Chop bounced onto the screen, looking like a ball of cotton with wiry little legs.

"This is my therapy dog, Lamby," Kristy continued. *"Therapy dogs help people by visiting with*

them. That helps tense people relax and can even make their blood pressure go down. The residents at Glenn Ridge love it when Lamby comes to see them. One man told me he feels like she's part of his family. And Lamby has a wonderful time there. She gets invited to all of the parties and sometimes provides entertainment."

Then there came the scene that Kristy had been working on in the editing bay, with a group of elderly people laughing and applauding. The camera then focused on Lamb Chop in her grass skirt, prancing around as a white-haired man strummed a ukulele. The camera followed Lamb Chop through other activities. There was a touching scene in which she hopped onto a bed and cuddled with the woman who lay there. After a moment, the woman reached up a fragile hand to stroke Lamb Chop's head.

"Lamby's one of a small group of therapy dogs who are allowed to get on the beds of sick people," Kristy said. *"That's because she's a Maltipoo and people aren't allergic to her."*

In the final scene, the woman on the bed started singing. Her voice was feeble, but true, and the song was a happy one.

"How much is that doggie in the window?" she crooned softly. *"The one with the waggly tail?"*

Andi's eyes filled with tears of sympathy as she listened.

Kristy's video ended, and suddenly, there she was on-screen, being interviewed by Mr. Donovan. He started by asking questions about therapy dogs, which Kristy answered quickly and easily. A therapy dog had to be over one year old, have all its shots, and be able to obey commands, she told him. Even more important, it had to be calm and well-behaved and enjoy socializing with strangers.

"That's Bebe!" Andi exclaimed. "She could be a therapy dog!"

"So could Lola!" Debbie cried, and then she reconsidered. "Maybe not. Lola doesn't obey very well."

"MacTavish is out," Tim said. "He's much too rowdy. He'd knock people out of their wheelchairs."

"Red wouldn't be right for that either," Bruce said regretfully. "He'd want to run up and down the halls."

Mr. Donovan continued his questions, and Kristy told him that a therapy dog's handler must be at least ten years old and that any handler under the age of sixteen had to be accompanied by a parent or a guardian.

"That's no problem for me," Kristy said. "My mom works at Glenn Ridge, so she's already there. Any time I bring Lamby, Mom's in the room with me."

Then Mr. Donovan asked if Lamb Chop would dance for them.

Lamb Chop didn't have to be asked twice. She was instantly up on her hind legs, twirling around, swishing her hula skirt in a professional manner, even though there wasn't any music. When her performance ended, she rushed to Kristy and leapt into her lap, wriggling with joy and self-satisfaction.

Lamb Chop was definitely a ham.

Then there was a break for a dog food commercial.

"I've got to admit, your girlfriend's cute," Tim told Bruce.

"She's not my girlfriend!" Bruce said a little too firmly. "She's just a good friend. A couple of weeks ago, you were calling her Jerry's girlfriend."

"I'm not saying that now," Tim said. "I saw your face while you were watching her cuddling Lamb

Chop. I'm your 'good friend,' and you don't look at *me* that way."

"She is too just a friend!" Andi said. "She's Bruce's friend, and my friend, and Aunt Alice's. Isn't that right, Aunt Alice?"

"I'm proud to claim Kristy as my friend," said Aunt Alice. "Especially after watching her conduct herself on television."

The commercials ended, and they returned their attention to the TV screen, where the title of Mr. Merlin's video appeared in gigantic letters — *GABBY TALKS*.

Technically, the video was nothing special. There was nothing on it but Gabby. He was sitting in a hard-back chair, staring apprehensively at the person behind the camera.

That person had the voice of Maynard Merlin.

"This is Gabby," he said. "He's a stray who turned up on my doorstep one day, and I decided to see if I could teach him to talk. I'd read a book about how to do that, and it didn't sound too hard — just a lot of time-consuming work. So I adopted Gabby and got him his shots and did the other stuff you have to do for a dog. My apartment became his classroom. Luckily, I had a small inheritance to live on, so I didn't have to leave the house to go to an outside job. I was free to work with Gabby from seven in the morning until seven at night, every day of the week. And under my expert tutorage, he did learn to talk. Right, Gabby?"

"Uh-huh," Gabby said, nodding.

"I already hate that man, and I can't even see him," Debbie said. "I just hate the sound of his voice." She spoke in a whisper so as not to drown out any of Gabby's comments.

"Okay, Gabby, let's chat," Mr. Merlin said. "Tell me about your life before you came to live with me. Was it easy or hard?"

"Harrrr," Gabby said. *D* was not one of the letters he could pronounce.

"Where did you get your food before I took you in?"

"Garagg cans," Gabby said, lowering his head in embarrassment.

"Were you happy eating out of garbage cans and living on the streets like a vagabond?" Mr. Merlin asked him.

"Uh-uh," Gabby said.

"Are you happier living with me, working hard to perfect your verbal skills?" Mr. Merlin asked.

"Uh-uh," Gabby said again.

"That is not the appropriate answer," Mr. Merlin said firmly. "The right answer is yes, but since dogs can't make the 's' sound, you need to say, 'Uh-huh,' to indicate that you mean yes. Can you do that, Gabby?"

"Uh-huh," Gabby said.

"Gabby says yes, he is very happy living with me," Mr. Merlin said. "Now, Gabby — "

"I can't bear to watch any more of this," Andi said. "Poor Gabby is being tortured! Twelve hours a day to teach him to say 'uh-huh'? Let's turn off the TV."

"No, dear," Aunt Alice said. "This is an eye-opener for all of us. Gabby is doing his best, and we need to see him through this. We also want to know what happened during his interview. That dog came out of the studio and collapsed in a chair. I personally thought he was having a nervous breakdown."

"Now, Gabby," Mr. Merlin continued, "why don't we sing a little song? You do like to sing, don't you?"

"Uh-huh," Gabby said, although he didn't seem to mean it.

"Let's make it a duet," Mr. Merlin said. He began to sing in an unpleasantly nasal voice. *"Twinkle, twinkle, little star!"*

"Wingle, wingle, liggle are!" Gabby sang. He was more on key than Mr. Merlin.

"Now, let's tell our viewers good-bye," Mr. Merlin said.

"Goowye," Gabby said with obvious relief.

Mercifully the video was over.

But Mr. Merlin and Gabby were *not* over. There was an abrupt transition to Star Burst Studios, where they were being interviewed by Mr. Donovan. Mr. Merlin was trying to elaborate on the challenges involved in teaching a dog to talk, but Mr. Donovan seemed more interested in what Gabby had to say.

"Are you enjoying your visit to Hollywood?" he asked Gabby.

"Uh-huh," Gabby answered.

"What part of it have you liked the best?" Mr. Donovan asked.

"Annie Wawar," Gabby said.

"That's me!" Andi gasped in delight. "The thing he liked best about being in Hollywood was *me!*"

"I have a request," Mr. Donovan said. "Do you enjoy receiving requests, Gabby?"

"Uh-uh," Gabby said.

"He means 'uh-huh,'" Mr. Merlin translated, shooting Gabby a disapproving look. "Gabby loves requests. What would you like for him to say?"

"What about reciting the Gettysburg Address?" Mr. Donovan suggested. "He probably hasn't memorized it, but I can recite it for him. 'Four score and seven years ago our fathers brought forth on this continent a new nation —'"

"Gabby can't recite that, Mr. Donovan!" Andi cried, forgetting for a moment that the man on the TV screen couldn't hear her. "Gabby can't make the 's' sound!"

"Or rore uh wenny ear awo," Gabby began courageously. Then he sighed and lowered his head to his paws.

"Try again, Gabby!" Mr. Merlin commanded angrily. "No one respects a quitter!"

"It's my fault," Mr. Donovan said quickly. "I asked for too much. It's just that the program will probably air sometime around the Fourth of July and I was hoping we might be able to include something patriotic."

"What about the national anthem?" Mr. Merlin

suggested. "Come on, Gabby, let's sing it together!" He began to sing: *"Oh, say can you see —"*

"That's not necessary," Mr. Donovan said hastily. "Our time is up now. Thanks so much to you both for appearing on our show. This has been an experience that I'm sure our viewers will never forget.

"Our phones are now open for call-in votes. Tune in tomorrow night, and we'll announce our winning dog. Will it be Lamb Chop Fernald from Elmwood, New Jersey? Or Gabby Merlin from Philadelphia, Pennsylvania? It's up to *you*, America!"

A phone number appeared at the bottom of the screen.

"Good-bye, everybody in television land!" Mr. Merlin cried, stepping in front of Mr. Donovan to beam into the camera lens. "What do you have to say to those nice people, Gabby?"

Gabby moaned, "Goowye."

CHAPTER FIFTEEN

They all called in to vote for Kristy's video.

That took quite a while, because the phone lines were so busy that it was hard to get through. Then, after all five of them had managed to cast their votes, Andi called in again and voted for *Gabby Talks*.

"How can you vote for that dreadful Mr. Merlin?" Debbie demanded.

"I'm not voting for *him*," Andi said. "I'm voting for Gabby. He'll feel like a failure if he doesn't receive a single vote."

"If you were going to vote for both of them, you might as well not have voted at all," Bruce said. "By voting for Gabby, you canceled out your vote for Kristy."

The following evening he was even more disgusted with her when Mr. Donovan announced that the winning video was *Gabby Talks*.

"The vote was extremely close," Mr. Donovan said, and Bruce glared at Andi.

"Your second vote may have sabotaged Kristy," he told her. "If you'd stuck with one vote like the rest of us, Lamb Chop might be going to Hollywood."

"No, she wouldn't," said Kristy. She had come over to the Walkers' house to watch the contest results with them and was curled up next to Bruce on the sofa. "I'd never let Lamby become a professional actor. I'm glad I didn't have to tell Mr. Donovan that I didn't want the prize. That would have been so embarrassing after everything he did for us."

"If you weren't hoping to win, then why did you enter?" Mrs. Walker asked with sincere interest.

This was the first time that Mr. and Mrs. Walker had met Kristy, and they both seemed surprised that she was sitting with Bruce instead of Andi.

"For the same reason Bruce and Andi entered *Bobby Strikes Back*," Kristy said. "I had a story I needed to tell. I'm glad I got into the finals, because now people all over the country know about therapy dogs and the valuable work they do. I just wish that *Bobby Strikes Back* had been shown, too. Then Red might have gone to Hollywood and become a movie star."

"I'd have said no to that, just like you would," Bruce said. "I'd never want Red to be under all that pressure. He's happy just being a normal dog."

"I predict that incredible Gabby has a great career ahead of him," Mr. Walker said. "I can picture him in dog food commercials saying, 'Yum! Yum! Yum!'"

"He would be great at that," Andi agreed. "He can say 'y' and 'm' and all of the vowels. 'Yum' would be a cinch for him. I hope the directors are good to him and don't make him try to say anything that has an 's' in it."

Her heart ached when she thought about Gabby's stunned expression when Mr. Donovan had requested the Gettysburg Address.

Remember what I told you when we said goodbye, she called out silently to Gabby, hoping her thoughts would cross the miles between them and enter his mind. It wasn't unreasonable to think that a dog who could talk might have psychic abilities as well.

The telephone rang. Since it was on a table next to where Andi was sitting, she was the one who answered it.

"I'd like to speak to Andrea Walker," a girl's voice said.

It wasn't a voice Andi recognized.

"I'm Andi Walker," she said.

The girl said, "Oh." Then there was silence. Andi wondered if the girl might be talking very softly and was being drowned out by the noise in the Walkers' family room. Not only was the TV still on, but Mr. and Mrs. Walker and Bruce and Kristy were involved in a spirited conversation about Gabby.

Andi carried the phone into the living room, where it was quieter.

There still was no sound from the phone except somebody's breathing.

After pausing another moment to give the caller a chance to identify herself, Andi asked, "Who is this?"

The girl at the other end of the line drew a long breath, as if she were preparing to dive into a deep lake and didn't know what she might find there.

"I've got something to tell you," she said. "First, though, you've got to promise that you'll never give my name to anybody or say where you got this information."

"I promise," Andi said readily. "Who are you?"

"My name is Sarah," the girl said. "I used to be Connor Gordon's girlfriend. He said he was crazy about me, and I believed him. Then, once he got what he wanted from me, he dropped me flat. On the night of the prom, he never came by to pick me up. I sat there, waiting and waiting, in my beautiful dress that cost me over one hundred dollars, and Connor didn't show. I called him on his cell, and he didn't answer. I called his house, and all I got was his mother's voice on their voice mail. I was scared that he'd been in a car wreck on the way over, so I started calling hospitals. Connor wasn't in any of their emergency rooms. I was out of my mind with worry!"

"I bet," Andi said. "Did you ever find out where he was?"

"He was at the prom with somebody else," Sarah said. "He and his date got crowned king and queen! On Monday, at school, he told me he'd forgotten he'd invited me and made me feel guilty because I hadn't reminded him. I was so upset that I threw my prom dress in a trash bin."

"That was dumb," Andi said. "You should have returned it to the store."

"I couldn't, because I'd sewed sequins on it," Sarah said.

"Then you should have given it to Goodwill."

Andi always hated to see things go to waste.

"You're right," Sarah said. "I was dumb to throw it away. I'm the stupidest person in the world. I never should have trusted Connor."

"Don't beat yourself up," Andi told her. "Everybody trusts Connor until he stabs them in the back. I'm sorry he broke your heart, but why are you calling me? I can't do anything about it."

"Because he's stabbed *you* in the back, too, and you don't even know it," Sarah said. "I was watching the *Eileen Stanton Show* the other night, and I learned about the contest for books about dogs. The boy who won first place looked exactly like Connor, except he was younger and didn't have a mustache. He had the same last name, so I figured they had to be related. Then some lady phoned in and said

Andrea Walker was the second-place winner and lived in Elmwood, New Jersey. That's how I was able to find your phone number."

"Why did you want my phone number?" Andi asked her.

"Because Jerry Gordon did not write *Ruffy Dean Joins the Circus*," Sarah said. "All he did was change the name of the dog and make up the title. The book's real title is *Tuffy Bean and the One-Ring Circus*. It's a very old book. Connor found a copy in a used-book store. He told me it was his mother's favorite book when she was a little girl and he wanted to give her a copy of the story for Mother's Day. The book was falling apart, so he asked me to retype it. I'm a very good typist, and it seemed like such a sweet thing for him to do for his mom that I said yes. It took me three weeks to type it. It wasn't a short book."

"It sure wasn't," Andi agreed, recalling the hefty manuscript that she had worked on for so long. She was beginning to catch the drift of where this conversation was headed, and was both excited and nervous. "So you gave your typed transcript to Connor?"

"I gave him the disk," Sarah said. "He seemed

so grateful! I honestly thought he was in love with me."

"Then he dumped you," Andi said in disgust. "On the night of the prom."

"I sat there waiting all evening in my beautiful dress," Sarah said, her voice quivering at the memory. "And my beautiful *shoes*. Did I tell you about my shoes? They're pink with purple sequins. I glued those on myself to go with the dress."

"Did you throw those away?" Andi asked.

This time she hoped that the answer would be yes. The shoes sounded awful.

"No," Sarah said. "I have other outfits they go with."

Andi restrained herself from pursuing the subject. She didn't want to know about the rest of Sarah's wardrobe.

"So Connor tricked you into copying the story," she said, summing things up. "Then he changed the title and sent the file to Jerry to print out and enter in the contest. Connor couldn't enter it himself, because he's over the age limit. Send me the book! That will give me the evidence to nail them!"

"I don't have the book," Sarah said. "Connor

took it back. I don't even remember who the author was. I was concentrating so hard on the typing — all that old-fashioned wording —"

She started to sob.

"Don't cry," Andi said. "You were brave and honest to call me. I respect you, Sarah. I think you're terrific. Really."

"You do?" Sarah sounded amazed. "Nobody's ever called me terrific before. Only Connor, when I gave him that disk."

"I'm not like Connor," Andi said. "I fib a little, but I never do it to hurt people. I know that's a fault of mine, and I'm going to correct it. I promised you that I wouldn't tell anyone you called me, but can we make one exception to that promise? I'd like to discuss this with my private investigator."

"You have a private investigator?" Sarah asked in astonishment. "I thought you were eleven years old!"

"I was eleven when I wrote my novel," Andi told her. "I've now turned twelve and am much more mature, and I do have a private investigator. She's totally trustworthy and keeps everything I tell her confidential. Please give me permission to tell her. We're in this together, aren't we, Sarah? You and I are partners on a quest for justice?"

Sarah was quiet for so long that Andi began to worry that she might have fainted from the stress of making this decision.

But Sarah surprised her.

"Go for it, Andi!" she said suddenly. "Tell your private investigator! I don't want that two-faced slimeball to get away with this! I just wish Connor had gotten arrested when Jerry did."

"Jerry got arrested?" Andi asked in surprise.

"When he and Connor were in New York together," Sarah said. "They used fake IDs to try to get into a nightclub. The bouncer recognized Jerry from the *Eileen Stanton Show*, so of course he knew his real age. Jerry's dad had to drive to New York to bail him out. Connor told everybody about it when he got home. He was so proud that he wasn't the one who got caught."

"Connor seems to be able to get away with anything," Andi said.

"That's why I don't want you leaking my name," Sarah told her. "He'll twist things around so people will think I'm the one who stole that story."

"Connor will never know you're a snitch," Andi promised. "Thank you for calling me, and I hope you enjoy your shoes. Purple sequins sound beautiful."

Andi swore to herself that this would be the last lie she would ever tell.

She clicked off the phone, clicked it on again, and punched in Aunt Alice's number. The phone rang eight times before she remembered that this was bingo night.

When Andi returned to the family room, the TV was off, and Bruce was helping Kristy get up from the sofa. That sight was surprising, since the sofa didn't sag, and Kristy normally bounced onto and off chairs like a rubber ball. Now, however, she let Bruce take her hand and pull her gently to her feet as if she were the heroine in an old-fashioned movie.

Once she was up, Bruce still didn't let go of her hand.

"Red and I are going to walk Kristy home," he said. "I'll be back in about an hour."

"An hour!" Mr. Walker exclaimed. "Where in the world does Kristy live — Florida?"

"Now, John," Mrs. Walker said soothingly. "It's

a beautiful moonlit night and it's good for them to walk slowly. We wouldn't want them running and tripping over curbs, would we? We enjoyed meeting you, Kristy. I'm sorry your video didn't win, but you seem to be handling the disappointment with maturity."

"I'm not disappointed," Kristy told her. "I'm happy for Gabby. This has been a really great evening."

"You can say that again!" Andi said with so much enthusiasm that everyone turned to stare at her.

She wished she could tell them about the phone call from Sarah.

She couldn't wait until morning, when she could tell Aunt Alice!

CHAPTER SIXTEEN

"Tuffy Bean!" Aunt Alice exclaimed. "That's a name I haven't heard for a long time. No wonder the name Ruffy Dean sounded so familiar. How silly of Connor to have stuck so closely to the original! Those Gordon boys are so arrogant that they don't even make the effort to cover their tracks."

"You mean you've heard of the Tuffy Bean circus book?" Andi asked her.

"There was a whole series of books about Tuffy," Aunt Alice said. "They were favorites of mine when I was a child. Let's see what we can find out about them on the Internet."

She switched on her computer and accessed her favorite search engine. Then she typed in the name Tuffy Bean. A page sprang up with a pen-and-ink drawing of a little black and white dog with a long skinny tail. He was dressed like a clown and was sitting on a barrel.

"There he is!" Aunt Alice said triumphantly. "That's Tuffy! Mr. Bean named him that because he was so tough. He never even yelped when he swallowed a bumblebee."

"That scene was in Jerry's manuscript!" Andi said. "I don't think Jerry even bothered to read the manuscript before he submitted it to the contest. He thought there were elephants in it, but it was only a traveling dog show."

"'*Tuffy Bean and the One-Ring Circus* by Leo Edwards was published in 1931,'" Aunt Alice read from the caption beneath the drawing. "That means the book is probably a collector's item. It was a fluke that Connor found a copy in a used-book store. I doubt very much that we'll find another one anywhere."

She started clicking links to online bookstores and typing in "Tuffy Bean." She got no hits.

The doorbell rang.

"Now, who could that be at ten in the morning?" Aunt Alice asked irritably. "Don't people realize they shouldn't come calling until noon? Here I am in my housecoat. How humiliating!"

She switched off the computer and hauled herself up from her chair. Followed closely by Andi, she went downstairs to the entrance hall and peered out through the peephole in the door.

"Oh, my!" she gasped. "Andi, please run and get my face mask. It's in the refrigerator. I like to keep it cold for when I wear it on hot days."

"Is somebody here with a dog?" Andi asked in surprise. She couldn't imagine anyone bringing a dog to visit Aunt Alice. All her friends were aware that she was allergic to them.

"It's a very nice dog," Aunt Alice responded as the bell chimed again. "But that doesn't make him less toxic. Hurry up, dear. His dander's wafting in through the keyhole."

Andi rushed to the kitchen and returned with the huge black mask, which had been resting next to a bowl of leftover salad. It smelled a little of onion.

The bell chimed insistently a third time, and Aunt Alice strapped on the mask. Then she pulled her dressing gown more tightly about her and opened the door.

There, on the doorstep, were Maynard Merlin and Gabby.

"What a surprise!" Aunt Alice exclaimed, although

of course she wasn't surprised at all, because she'd already seen them. "What are the two of you doing here in Elmwood?"

"Actually, I drove here just to see you," Mr. Merlin said. "The time we spent together in Hollywood was so memorable that I haven't been able to get you out of my mind. I got here last night and immediately tried to call you, but there was no answer, so I stayed at a motel. I waited to come over this morning until I was sure you would be up and about."

"I'm up," Aunt Alice said, "but not exactly 'about' yet. Since you're here, you might as well come in and sit down. Please don't take this personally, Gabby, but I'd prefer that you stay in the entrance hall. Even a clean, short-haired dog might shed on the furniture."

"Gabby, stay," Mr. Merlin commanded sternly.

Gabby slumped into a dejected heap on the floor. However, his sad eyes brightened when he saw Andi.

"Hi, Gabby!" she said, hugging him. "It's so good to see you!"

Gabby didn't say anything, but his lips curled up in what Andi thought was a smile.

"What a lovely home you have, Alice!" Mr. Merlin said, glancing approvingly about the well-furnished living room. "And your garden out front is lovely too. You're obviously a dedicated homemaker and apparently financially secure."

"What, may I ask, is the reason for this visit?" Aunt Alice inquired, taking a seat in a chair and motioning Mr. Merlin to the sofa.

"As I said, you've been on my mind since we met," Mr. Merlin said. "I was hoping that perhaps your romantic situation might have changed and you would have become available. But I see you're still wearing the mask that symbolizes your betrothal."

"Nothing has changed in my life," Aunt Alice told him. "But obviously things have changed in *yours*. I was busy last night and was unable to watch the results of the video contest, but Andi has told me that *Gabby Talks* was the winner. Congratulations! I'm sure you and Gabby are thrilled. Have film offers started rolling in yet?"

"Yes, indeed," Mr. Merlin told her. "Those started even before the results were announced. Gabby already has received offers to appear in four TV commercials, and three well-known agents want to represent him. I've had a call from a big hotel in Las Vegas that wants to book him for a four-week engagement in November. He's also received a request to appear on the *Eileen Stanton Show*."

"That's wonderful," Aunt Alice said politely.

"It would be if Gabby hadn't stopped talking," Mr. Merlin said.

"Really?" Aunt Alice glanced at Gabby in the entrance hall. Andi was on the floor next to him, scratching behind his ears. He looked contented.

"It was after we taped that interview for Star Burst Studios," Mr. Merlin said. "Gabby hasn't said a single word since. Not even last night, when we were watching TV in our motel room and Mr. Donovan announced that our video had won. I yelled, 'Hooray!' and Gabby should have shouted, 'Oooray!' right along with me. But he didn't say anything. He just lay down on the floor and went to sleep."

"Perhaps he's resting his vocal cords," Aunt Alice suggested.

"I wish that were true, but it's something more serious," Mr. Merlin said. "I've tried everything — threatening him, bribing him, punishing him — "

"You beat poor Gabby because he stopped talking?" Andi cried.

"Of course not," Mr. Merlin assured her. "I'm not a monster. I just made him stand in the corner and have 'time out.' He doesn't like that, and it's usually enough to get him rolling. But not this time. The dog's gone mute. He's totally useless. We're receiving all these offers that could make me rich for life, and I can't take advantage of them. You can't imagine how infuriating and frustrating that is!"

"It's a pity," Aunt Alice agreed. "But Gabby still has his sweet personality. I'm sure you enjoy his company even if he isn't as chatty as he once was."

"I have no use for a dog who doesn't earn his keep," Mr. Merlin said. "Having to feed and walk him is more trouble than it's worth. Perhaps your future husband would like to buy him for you as a wedding gift? If not, I'm afraid I'm going to have to take him to the pound."

"You can't do that!" Andi cried from her seat in the entrance hall. "You can't adopt a dog and then throw him away!"

"This is Gabby's decision," Mr. Merlin said. "I've described to him what the pound is like and how animals are crammed into cages and how sad it is for them when they don't get adopted. And I've told him how much money he'll earn in Hollywood and how I'll accompany him there as his trainer and be paid as well. He doesn't listen. He just stares off into space. One time he even growled at me! He's not supposed to growl, he's supposed to talk."

"I'd love to take Gabby, but I'm afraid that's impossible," said Aunt Alice.

"I don't see why." Mr. Merlin gestured about him at the spacious living room. "You seem to be fond of Gabby and have plenty of space to keep a pet, while I live in a small apartment that can't possibly accommodate two dogs."

"Two dogs?" Andi exclaimed. "I thought Gabby was your only dog."

"He is at the moment," Mr. Merlin told her. "But since Gabby is no longer talking, I plan to get another dog and immediately start training it. It will have to be a rush job, but I can't let all these high-pay opportunities go to waste. I'll have to intensify the training and allow fewer potty breaks, but now that I've developed my teaching techniques, I can probably get my new dog ready within a year. But not with Gabby lazing around, doing nothing. What kind of example would that be for his replacement?"

"As I said, I would happily take Gabby if I could," Aunt Alice said. "However, I must confess with a bit of embarrassment that I have misled you about the reason for this face mask. It has nothing to do with cultural betrothal traditions. It's an allergy mask. I am terribly allergic to dogs."

Mr. Merlin regarded her accusingly.

"You *lied* to me, Alice!"

"I most certainly did not," Aunt Alice said. "I dissembled. You chose to believe that this mask meant one thing, and I didn't attempt to dissuade you, because I didn't want to encourage your attentions. The truth, Mr. Merlin, is that there are things about you that are of concern to me. I don't like the way you treat Gabby, and I have some problems with your marital history. You've had almost as many wives as King Henry the Eighth."

"How would you know how many wives I've had?" Mr. Merlin demanded.

"Aunt Alice is a private investigator," Andi told him.

"You're joking, of course?" Mr. Merlin said. But he was starting to look nervous.

"Indeed she is not," said Aunt Alice. "And now, Mr. Merlin, I do think it's time that you left. It's a long drive back to Philadelphia."

"No!" Andi cried, wrapping her arms around Gabby. "He can't take Gabby to the pound! Mr. Merlin, please let me adopt him!"

"Be my guest," Maynard Merlin said sullenly, getting to his feet. "I can't imagine why you'd want him, but it will save me a trip to the pound."

"I hope you won't mind if I don't see you out," said Aunt Alice. "I'd hate for the neighbors to see me ushering a man out of my home as I stand in the doorway in my dressing gown."

"I'm perfectly capable of letting myself out," snarled Mr. Merlin. "And you can tell your fiancé that he has my sympathy."

Once his car had rumbled out of the driveway, Aunt Alice said, "Andi, I understand your reason for acting impulsively, but are you sure your parents will welcome another dog?"

"Probably not, but I'll talk them into it," Andi said. "I couldn't let Gabby suffer because of me."

"Because of you?" Aunt Alice repeated in bewilderment. "Dear, you are not responsible for this dog's not talking."

"But I am!" Andi cried. "As I was saying goodbye to him, I whispered, 'Take control of your life! Don't let anybody force you to talk unless you want to.' Gabby listened to me, didn't you, Gabby?"

Gabby barked.

CHAPTER
SEVENTEEN

Her parents agreed to the adoption with so little argument that Andi was stunned. One reason was that while Andi, Bruce, Tim, and Debbie had been watching the Star Burst show at Aunt Alice's house, Mr. and Mrs. Walker had been watching at home.

Both had been shocked by Mr. Merlin's description of Gabby's training program.

"That poor dog deserves some rest and relaxation," Mrs. Walker said sympathetically. "He needs to live in a loving home."

Gabby smiled. Now that he had stopped talking, he had become very good at smiling. He stretched his big lips to both sides and turned them up at the corners whenever anybody said something nice to him.

Even Mr. Walker, who had stated over and over,

"Two dogs are more than enough for any one family," had melted at the sight of Gabby's smile.

"If it's us or the pound, then it has to be us," he said.

Red Rover, who had gotten to know Gabby during their time together in Hollywood, seemed delighted to renew their friendship and watched with interest as Tim helped Bruce build a second doghouse in the Walkers' backyard.

The only member of the family who was not happy was Bebe, who went into a snit at the thought of having to share her mistress's affections with an outsider.

Andi considered telling her that Gabby was Aunt Alice's dog and was only there to visit while Aunt Alice was out of town. Then she reminded herself that she had given up lying. Lies had a way of catching up with you. Her statement to Mr. Donovan that Jerry's hand had been smashed in a garbage disposal had caused her a lot of embarrassment.

Also, Bebe was no dummy. She knew quite well that Aunt Alice was allergic to dogs.

So Andi told Bebe the truth while she held and cuddled her.

"You will always be special, because you belonged to me first," she told Bebe. "But Gabby is special too, in a different way."

Bebe sulked for a while, but seemed to feel better when she realized that Gabby would be sleeping in the backyard. Andi's bedroom closet was not large enough to conceal two dogs.

The rest of summer vacation disappeared as quickly as toilet paper when you got near the end of the roll. There seemed to be so much left, and then, suddenly, it was gone, and you couldn't even remember using it up.

Mrs. Walker took the children shopping for school clothes, and Andi discovered that she had graduated from the children's department to the juniors. More startling still, Bruce had to buy jeans in the men's department. They were the smallest jeans on the rack, and he had to wear a belt to keep them up, but he needed the extra length.

Over the summer, Bruce had gotten his growth spurt.

Elmwood Middle School was very different from Elmwood Elementary. Andi found that both exciting and disorienting. There was a different teacher for each subject, and there were armloads of books to carry around, and she had a locker with a combination lock that she could never remember how to open. Arithmetic was called math, and instead of recess, there was P.E., where they had to do jumping jacks and learn to climb a rope. Bells kept ringing, and messages blared over a loudspeaker.

The whole experience was so chaotic that it made Andi's head spin.

But there were good things, too. The best was the Creative Writing Club. Andi and Debbie had both joined that as soon as they had learned about it — Debbie because she had written the gossip column for *The Bow-Wow News* and considered herself a journalist, and Andi because she had been longing for such a group all her life. She felt certain her future husband was a member of the club and would eventually emerge and reveal himself. She wasn't in a hurry for that to happen, because it would spoil the suspense, and besides, she wouldn't need a boyfriend for at least three years. There wouldn't be any proms until she got to high school, and she wasn't sure she'd want to go to one even then. The thought of Sarah's purple-sequined shoes was a definite turnoff.

One Saturday morning, a few weeks after school had started, Andi was in her bedroom, working on a project for the Creative Writing Club, when Bruce rapped on her door and said, "Kristy's here."

"So what's new?" Andi called back, irritated by being interrupted at a point where words were coming easily and her story was starting to take shape. "It seems like Kristy is always here."

She still liked Kristy but was getting a little tired of her. Ever since the night when Bruce had walked Kristy home and had *not* come back in an hour like he had said he would, Kristy had been at the Walker house so constantly that she had become as familiar as the furniture. All Bruce's free time, except when he was eating or taking Red for a run, was spent doing something with Kristy. They were always working together on a photography project or studying together at the kitchen table or watching TV in the family room. Even at school, when Andi caught sight of her brother in the hall between classes, he and Kristy were usually walking together, hand in hand, like Hansel and Gretel on their way to the gingerbread house.

"She wants to talk to you about something," Bruce said now.

"About what?" Andi asked him through the door.

"Come out and find out for yourself," Bruce told her.

So Andi set her notebook aside and reluctantly went downstairs, where Kristy was waiting in the entrance hall.

"Hi, Andi," Kristy said. "I've got a favor to ask you. There's a very old man, Mr. Sherman, who lives at Glenn Ridge, and his mind is sort of wandering. He drifts back and forth between now and when he was a kid. He keeps talking about a dog named Silver that he had when he was seven years old. He must have had a lonely childhood. He talks about Silver as if he was his only friend."

"That's sad," Andi said. The idea of it made her uneasy. She didn't like to imagine how it would be to get so old that you couldn't tell the past from the present. Aunt Alice was old, but that hadn't happened to her. Andi prayed it never would.

"My mom thinks a therapy dog visit might help him," Kristy said.

"So you're going to take Lamb Chop?" Andi asked.

"I tried that," Kristy said. "Mr. Sherman didn't like Lamby. He said when he put his hand on her, it was like petting a mop. That hurt Lamby's feelings."

"I'm sure it did," Andi said. She knew how easily Bebe's feelings got hurt, and Lamb Chop was probably even more sensitive. After all, she was used to having everyone adore her.

"The way Mr. Sherman describes him, I think Silver must have looked a lot like Gabby," Kristy said. "He was sort of a hound, but not purebred, and had floppy ears and short, smooth hair. Will you come with us to take Gabby to meet Mr. Sherman? Bruce says Gabby won't go without you."

"I'm not old enough to be his handler," Andi reminded her. "Neither is Bruce. We'd have to be sixteen."

"Not if a parent or guardian comes with you," Kristy said. "I already asked your mom, and she said she'd be glad to. She told me that ever since she saw my video, she's been thinking that this might be a good thing for you and her to start doing together."

"She was probably thinking about taking Bebe," Andi said. "Bebe loves being with people. She'd be a great therapy dog."

"She would," Kristy agreed. "But she wouldn't be right for Mr. Sherman. Mr. Sherman is dreaming about a hound. If he didn't like Lamby, he won't like Bebe. Even with floppy ears, she's still definitely a dachshund."

"Come on, Andi," Bruce coaxed. "It won't take long. Then you can go back to your writing or whatever you were doing. Mom's outside in the car, but Gabby's acting stubborn. When I told him we wanted to take him for a ride, he ran into his doghouse."

"I told him he doesn't have to do anything he doesn't want to do," Andi said.

"Then make him *want* to do it," Bruce said impatiently. "He'll listen to you, but he doesn't seem to trust me. He's scared, but I don't know why. And of course he won't tell me."

"Please, Andi, try," Kristy said. "This could mean so much to Mr. Sherman. He doesn't have any family or friends to visit him. All he has are memories of his dog."

"Okay, I'll go talk to Gabby," Andi said. "But I'm not going to pressure him. If he doesn't want to go to Glenn Ridge, he shouldn't have to do it."

When she opened the kitchen door to go into the backyard, Red came racing to greet her. If only Mr. Sherman's childhood pet had been a setter! Red was always eager to go anywhere with anyone, unless, of course, it was Jerry.

"Not this time, Red," Andi told him, pausing a moment to run a hand over his silky head. Then she went to Gabby's doghouse and knelt down to peer in at him. His nose was between his paws, and his eyes held a look of desperation.

Andi knew at once what the problem was.

"You don't have to worry about going to the pound," she assured him. "You belong to us. This is your home now. Red and Bebe are your brother and sister. You're never going to see Mr. Merlin again, and we're never going to give you away. Even if you do something naughty like pee on the carpet or throw up a strawberry sundae, we're going to keep you forever. Do you understand?"

Gabby raised his head and stared up into her face. He seemed to be trying to decide whether to believe her.

Then, slowly, he inched his way out of his doghouse and stood up.

"We're going to visit a man named Mr. Sherman," Andi told him. "Then we're going to come back home."

She got to her feet and started across the yard. Gabby fell into step beside her.

Mr. Sherman was alone in his room. It was a sterile room with no pictures on the walls, no books on the shelves, and no potted plants on the window ledge. He sat in a wheelchair with his back to the window. He wasn't reading or working on a crossword puzzle. He was simply sitting there.

The door to the hall stood open.

"Who's that?" he asked anxiously when Kristy rapped on the door frame and stepped into the room.

"It's me," Kristy told him. "Kristy Fernald. Remember the other day when I brought my dog, Lamby, to see you, and you didn't like her because she felt like a mop?"

"Did I say that?" Mr. Sherman seemed bewildered. "Maybe I did. I certainly don't like mops."

"I've brought some visitors today that you might like better," Kristy said. "My boyfriend, Bruce; his mom, Mrs. Walker; and his sister, Andi."

"I'm glad to meet you, Mr. Sherman," Mrs. Walker said gently. Her eyes grew soft as she gazed at the man in the wheelchair.

Bruce and Andi both said, "Hello," but it was obvious that Mr. Sherman wasn't listening. He was in a world of his own.

"So where's the mop?" he demanded.

"She's at home," Kristy said. "I didn't bring her today."

"That's good," Mr. Sherman said. "So why are you here? If you didn't bring me Silver, it's not worth coming here."

"We did bring a dog to visit you," Kristy told him.

"What kind of a dog?" Mr. Sherman demanded. "Some yappy thing with a tassel on its tail? The only dog I give a darn about is Silver."

That was when Andi realized that Mr. Sherman was blind.

Kristy motioned her forward.

Take Gabby to him, she mouthed. She didn't speak the words aloud because Mr. Sherman's hearing seemed to be fine and he wasn't eager to be introduced to another strange dog. He wanted Silver, the dog he had loved in his childhood.

Andi took Gabby by the collar and led him to the wheelchair. Gabby laid his head on Mr. Sherman's lap.

The old man responded to the weight on his knees by reaching down to see what was there. It was the head of a dog that his hands and his heart remembered.

He slid his hands over Gabby's sleek head, fingered the long floppy ears and the soft rolls of jowls beneath the strong jaw. He bent forward to run his hand down the long smooth back, almost to the root of the tail. Then he returned his hands to the head in his lap. He cradled that head as if it were a precious jewel.

"Hello, old friend," he said softly. "I've missed you so much!"

Gabby said, "Allo."

CHAPTER EIGHTEEN

Andi had just arrived home from a Creative Writing Club meeting when she saw an envelope with the return address of Pet Lovers Press lying in the entrance hall under the mail slot. This time her name was spelled correctly.

As before, she didn't immediately open the envelope, but it wasn't because she wanted to prolong the excitement. She wasn't excited at all. She felt sure it contained an invitation to enter the Young Author Cat Lovers Contest.

She picked up the envelope and carried it into the kitchen, where she laid it on the counter while she made two tuna sandwiches, one for herself and one for her dogs. She cut the second sandwich in two and placed one of the halves in Bebe's bowl. Then she carried the other half into the backyard to give to Gabby.

As she'd hoped, Red Rover wasn't there. Bruce, who had not been delayed by an after-school activity, must have taken Red running. That was a relief, because since Gabby and Red were now practically roommates, Andi was finding it difficult to give Gabby the same treats she gave Bebe while withholding those treats from Red. Bruce was very strict about Red's diet and wouldn't allow him to eat people food.

Life in a multidog family was not always easy.

While Gabby wolfed down his sandwich and Andi ate hers, she finally got around to opening her letter.

When she saw the first paragraph, she couldn't believe what she was reading.

Dear Ms. Andrea Walker,

The first-place winner in our Young Author Dog Lovers Contest has been disqualified.

This means that your delightful novel, Bobby Strikes Back, *has been promoted from second place and become our grand-prize winner. If, in the intervening months, you have not sold your story elsewhere, we would very much like to publish it.*

Please let us know if Bobby Strikes Back *is still available.*

Sincerely,

Jo Ann Bayse, Senior Editor

Pet Lovers Press

Andi read the letter once and then read it a second time.

She bolted across the yard, out through the gate, into the alley, and down the sidewalk to Aunt Alice's house. She didn't even pause to ring the doorbell. She just threw open the door and rushed right in.

"Aunt Alice!" she cried. "My book is going to be published!"

Aunt Alice was seated in her favorite chair, sipping tea and reading a romance novel.

"Wipe your feet, dear," she said. "I just had the carpets cleaned. I wondered how long it would take for Jerry to be disqualified."

"How did you do it?" Andi asked her. "What did you tell them? You knew I promised not to tell anyone about Sarah!"

"I used alternative methods," Aunt Alice said. "I kept searching the Internet and finally found a Web site called Ugly Bird Books. They actually had a copy of *Tuffy Bean and the One-Ring Circus.* Only one copy, but that was all we needed. And they only charged me three dollars."

"Ugly Bird Books?" Andi repeated.

"A wonderful Web site," Aunt Alice said. "They gave an honest description of the book. Poor condition hardcover. Some torn and stained pages. A missing jacket. Some very old, very hard peanut butter smeared in the margins. But it was the same dear book I remembered from my childhood. I ordered it online and had them ship it directly to Pet Lovers Press. I hoped the editor would be able to put two and two together. Apparently she did."

"I'm going to be a published author!" Andi said softly. The idea was so overwhelming she could hardly take it in. "*Bobby Strikes Back* is going to be in bookstores! It's going to be in libraries! Teachers will put it on reading lists for their students!"

"And you'll probably be asked to give interviews," Aunt Alice said. "It's nice that you'll have an experienced consultant to advise you."

"You can't mean Jerry!" Andi exclaimed incredulously.

"Certainly not," said Aunt Alice. "I was referring to Gabby. With all the embarrassment this sham must be causing the Gordons, Jerry will probably be grounded for at least two days.

"On the subject of Gabby, I received a wedding announcement from Maynard Merlin. He enclosed a photo of himself and his lovely bride, Medusa. Mr. Merlin had a bandage on his hand. Gabby's replacement may not be as docile as Gabby."

"Did you run a background check on Medusa?" Andi asked her.

"Well, yes," Aunt Alice confessed, looking slightly embarrassed. "That wasn't exactly ethical, but I couldn't restrain myself. Medusa has had six husbands and owns a pit bull. We don't need to worry about her."